Silver Charms

Silver Charms

Kate Moseman

Silver Charms

First Edition
ISBN 978-1-7345144-6-9 (ebook)
ISBN 978-1-7345144-7-6 (paperback)

Published by:
Fortunella Press

In some cases I quite like irritating people who need to be irritated.

—Robert Smith

1

Fire leaped from the tip of my finger to the rolled-up newspaper stuffed under the coals. The paper caught and burned with a cheerful glow. Who needs lighter fluid when you have fire magic?

My oversized foster dog, Braveheart, lifted his big brown head. Curiosity lit his eyes—probably hoping the lighting of the grill portended meat in his future. When food didn't immediately materialize, he lowered his head to rest on his paws.

The kindling burned, but it would take time for the coals to settle into a deep glow. I didn't feel any need to rush the process. The back of the cabin faced uninterrupted upland Florida forest—I could sit under the slash pines, listening to the mockingbirds, until the moon plunged the forest into sharp relief, if I so pleased. I settled into a weathered Adirondack chair to wait.

Some people—the type that don't mind their own business—have asked me how I can stand to live all alone out here in my little old cabin in the woods. The truth is I *like* living alone. Well, all alone except for Braveheart. Whenever the world is too much, I retreat to my cabin for peace and quiet and all the benefits of a life unencumbered.

I held my hands before me and let silver flames dance from fingertip to fingertip. The sight never failed to bring me a sense of satisfaction. I curled my fingers into fists and extinguished the flames. Fire on, fire off. Like the Karate Kid, minus Mr. Miyagi.

Braveheart lifted his head and thumped his tail just before I heard the crunch of wheels in the driveway on the other side of the house.

I stood. I wasn't expecting anyone, and the twisty dirt road that led to my home rarely saw any accidental traffic.

The slam of a car door carried from the front of the house, followed by the sound of footsteps on the hollow wooden steps leading to the raised front porch.

Probably my friends, Luella and Pepper, wanting to practice their magic—air and water, respectively—or perhaps I'd let it slip that I was cooking ribs. If that was the case, I'd be lucky if there were any ribs left for me and Braveheart after those two got hold of them.

I walked around the corner of the cabin and down the stepping stone footpath to the front. Overgrown palmettos and skinny, twisted oaks obscured my view of the driveway until I was just a few feet away from it.

I froze, my bare toes curling into cool, sandy soil. The vehicle that had pulled up wasn't Luella's car or Pepper's

SUV. It was a white Lincoln Town Car I'd only seen once before—and I'd never forget that night.

The car's engine purred. That meant there was still some-one in the car—the chauffeur, no doubt—and someone else, someone I very much did not want to see, standing on my porch. Someone who was now pounding on the front door like she owned it.

I ignited balls of fire in both hands and stalked across the sand, then jumped onto the porch from the side. She may have owned half of Sparkle Beach, but she damn well didn't own my cabin—or me. I brandished the silver flames. "Hey!"

It may not have been the best opening salvo, but it certainly got her attention.

The woman on my front porch pivoted smartly on her classic pumps. Her iron-gray bob didn't budge a millime-ter, nor did her expression, which remained stuck on pure disapproval as her imperious gaze swept from my bare feet to my black hair. "Don't be a show-off, Rose."

"Don't call me 'Rose' like we're friends."

"Do you prefer Miss Conleth?"

I ignored the sarcasm. "After what you did to my friend and her boyfriend, I'd rather you not call me anything at all. Or show up at my house."

Her prim mouth tightened further. She smoothed the front of her power suit as if I had somehow rumpled it by looking at it. "That is ancient history. Luella is safe and sound, and living in a fine house given to her by me." She waved a hand in dismissal. "We have important things to discuss, you and I. So put away the flames and let's get on with it."

I pushed the flames to burn larger. They rocketed from my fingertips like tiny blowtorches. "What makes you think I would do that, Hilda?" I knew she hated being called by her first name.

She narrowed her eyes. "That's Mrs. Millefleur, to you."

I matched her stare for stare. My friends tell me I have a knack for it. "Is that supposed to intimidate me? I'm the one with the firepower now. The only magic you have left is hypnotizing people, and that won't work on me." Technically, I didn't know that for sure—but sometimes a bluff is as good as a fact.

"If it weren't for you—"

If it weren't for you meddling kids. The words from Scooby-Doo sprang to mind, absurdly, as if Luella, Pepper and I were youngsters rather than middle-aged women. "If it weren't for us you'd still have your fire magic? As far as I can tell, Sparkle Beach and the world in general is better off that way."

Mrs. Millefleur closed her eyes and released a sharp sigh. "I'm not trying to get it back. And I have no desire to hypnotize you, as appealing as that option may be in contrast to trying to teach a foolish, argumentative woman."

I lowered my hands. "Teach?"

Her gaze flicked to the door. "Could we possibly continue this conversation inside like civilized people?"

Braveheart bounded around the corner and heaved himself onto the porch with a thumping clatter, trailing a thin strand of dog drool onto the wooden boards as he righted himself.

Mrs. Millefleur made a strangled noise and backed up against the front door as if she could hide in the doorframe. "Get away!"

I glanced at Braveheart, who sat down and industriously scratched his flank with a back paw. "What, him? He's just an old softy. Wouldn't hurt a fly." I paused. "Unless he thought I was being threatened." That bluff was so big my nose should have grown. Braveheart would have sold me out for a scratch behind the ears.

She pressed herself even harder against the door. The unlocked latch gave way with a snap, and she stumbled backward across the threshold and into the cabin.

Braveheart happily pursued his new friend.

I hastily extinguished my fire and ran inside to find Mrs. Millefleur standing on my couch, her sensible heels about to punch holes in the cushions. "Get down before you ruin my couch!"

"Call him off!"

Braveheart danced and dodged like we were playing an exciting new game.

I rolled my eyes. "Braveheart, sit."

He sat.

"Good boy." I patted his head and ran my hand over his furry back. Being a part-time dog trainer really comes in handy in certain circumstances. I eyed the intruder. "Mrs. Millefleur, sit."

Without taking her eyes off the dog, she gingerly lowered herself and sat on the couch.

"Now state your business."

She folded and refolded her hands, then glanced at the blackened fireplace—a consequence of the earliest manifestation of my fire powers—before speaking. "I've come to teach you."

I laughed. "You're joking."

"I am not." Her voice shifted from command to statement as her gaze dropped to the floor.

"I don't need your help."

Her hands tightened and released. "Your friend Luella has her mother to teach her the ways of air magic. Pepper's boss, Queenie, will teach her water magic. You have no one."

"I don't need anyone, either."

"Don't be a fool, Rose."

"I'd be a fool to get involved with you. Look what you already did."

Her head snapped up. "I had my reasons."

Braveheart barked and ran to the front door.

Mrs. Millefleur's gaze followed his movement.

Multiple car doors slammed in quick succession. I smirked. "I bet that's Luella and Pepper. I don't fancy your chances with them. I wonder what they'll do to you when they catch you here trying to throw your weight around?" I stalked to the front window and peeked out, expecting to see my best friends alighting from Pepper's SUV. Instead, I saw a hybrid sedan and a tall woman in a hippie skirt herding two long-limbed girls toward the porch.

My heart stopped. That certainly wasn't Luella and Pepper.

It was my sister and her daughters—who never, ever made an unplanned visit—and they were carrying what appeared to be overnight bags.

I whirled on my unwanted guest and forced my expression into what I hoped was a semblance of calm. "Leave. Now. Out the back."

She didn't budge. "Why?"

I almost growled. I didn't need any further complications in my life right now on top of whatever was about to walk through my door.

Hilda stood, as cool as spring water, and crossed the room to peek out the curtains. "Just tell whoever it is that I'm a friend. I'll wait for you to send them away."

"I'm not telling her you're my—" Footsteps thumped on the raised porch, derailing my train of thought. "And I'm not sending them away."

The doorbell rang.

I glared at Mrs. Millefleur. The last thing I wanted was a collision between my family life and my witch life. I made a snap decision, for better or worse. "Fine, *friend*. But say nothing."

She pantomimed zipping her lips and throwing away the key.

I whipped the door open. "Isabella! How lovely to see you and the girls! Come in, come in."

"Hello!" Isabella glided in, the hem of her full bohemian-style skirt swishing just above the floor. She hugged me, smelling of eucalyptus and tea tree oil like she always did.

Her daughters trailed in behind her, shifting their bags to balance the weight as they crossed the threshold. Astrid, the oldest one—the one who looked the most like me—tucked her green-and-black ombre hair behind her ears and furrowed her brow. Sadie—the younger one, with her mother's flower child look—took in the scene with wide-eyed interest.

Isabella cleared her throat. "Girls, why don't you put your bags down and take Braveheart for a little walk around the back?"

"He's just been out—" I stopped at the meaning-filled look on my sister's face and recalculated the rest of the sentence. "I mean, he's *just been dying* to get outside." I scooped up the nearest leash and handed it to Astrid.

Astrid clipped the leash on Braveheart's collar and shot all of us one last dubious look before leading her younger sister and the dog out the back door.

Isabella exhaled and swept her gaze over Mrs. Millefleur.

I took the cue. "This is Hilda. She was just leaving—weren't you, Hilda?"

Mrs. Millefleur's face froze in a look that was half smile, half murder. "I'll be back." Her hawkish eyes glittered.

I swallowed the *not if I can help it* that was on my lips, and forced a smile. "I'll be ready for you."

She met my gaze with a controlled burn in her eyes, then turned to Isabella. "I didn't catch your name, miss...?"

"Isabella." She smiled uncertainly, catching the tension between Mrs. Millefleur and me, but not understanding it. "I'm Rose's sister."

Mrs. Millefleur's gaze traveled between the two of us, obviously making a comparison: me, black-haired and black-clothed, looking like a thief on the job; Isabella, henna-haired and draped with billowing earth-toned fabrics. Delicate silver jewelry with an almost elven sensibility completed Isabella's look, whereas my jewelry consisted of tiny skull earrings, a charm bracelet of tiny silver knives, and a pendant of a skull with a knife in it. "I didn't know Rose had a sister. It's a pleasure to meet you."

Isabella echoed the polite phrase, and capped it with a strained smile that said *please leave now.*

I opened the door and waited for Mrs. Millefleur to clear the porch before I shut the door and locked it. I watched out the window to make sure she drove away, then I turned to face my sister. "What the hell is going on, Izzy?"

2

Instead of answering me, Isabella retreated down the hall to the back door.

I threw my hands up and followed her. "Izzy?"

She peered through the sliver where the curtain didn't quite cover the window. Outside, the girls had Braveheart well in hand, and the trio seemed content to pace the sandy backyard.

"They're fine," I said.

She sighed and turned to face me. "I know. I just wanted to make sure they couldn't hear me." Her expression aged her face far more than the few years that separated us.

I gripped her shoulders, giving her a little shake. "What is going on?"

"Damon is driving me up the wall. I needed a break."

Of course it was Damon. They were in the process of divorcing, but still living under the same roof—a complete nightmare by anyone's standards. The overnight bags the girls had dropped on the floor loomed in my peripheral vision. "What do you mean, a *break*?"

"You know the divorce can't be settled until we finish negotiating over the house. But now that he's decided he wants it, he's making life difficult."

"What? Why?"

"Because, for some reason, he thinks if he can get me to leave the house, he'll have an edge in the negotiation."

I stared at her. "So why are you here, if that gives him an edge?"

"I told you. I *need* a break. He's insufferable!"

"Define insufferable."

"He can't possibly be an adult about this—oh, no. He has to drop hints about chatting with women on hookup apps. And what he'll do to the house once he has it to himself. Plus little digs about how I won't make enough money without him. All while leaving a trail of destruction like he usually does."

Visions of murder by fire floated through my head. I took a slow, deep breath and blew it out. "But if you abandon the house …"

"I'm not abandoning it, okay? It's just a little break. A little Damon-free vacation."

"Since when do you have the money for that?"

Izzy looked at me with puppy eyes.

My brow furrowed. She knew I didn't have money, either. Everything I had went into paying off the cabin early. I frowned—then I put two and two together, and I didn't much like the solution. "You want to stay *here*?"

"Just for a day or two? Please? To clear my head? I'll owe you a plant. You can start your own garden," she added hopefully.

I squeezed my eyes shut and reopened them. The Advil in the bathroom cabinet was calling my name. "I am the death of plants. You know that."

She said nothing, but widened her eyes to look even more like a sad cartoon puppy.

I pretended to glare at her. "Fine. But only for a day or two. You have to go back before he has any leverage to say you don't want the house."

Izzy threw her arms around me. "You're the best big sister ever."

"You're killing me," I said, but I hugged her tight. After a moment, my shoulder felt wet. I patted her back. "Do you want me to murder Damon? Because I will, you know." Isabella had no idea I had magic powers and that I could follow through on my threat in an assortment of creative ways.

She nodded against my shoulder and let out a weak laugh. "What do you do when someone is trying to burn your whole life down?"

A grim smile threatened at the corners of my lips. If anyone was going to burn it all down, it was going to be me. Damon had no idea who he was messing with. I carefully released Izzy so I could look her in the eye. "You can't stay here forever, but that doesn't mean I can't help you in other ways."

"Like what?" She knuckled the corners of her eyes and sniffed.

"Aren't you the one who's always telling me the universe will provide?"

Izzy made a hiccuping sound. "I don't know if I believe that anymore. You always said that was ridiculous. That people were trash. Maybe you were right."

Being right tasted like a mouthful of ashes. "No, you're *still* right. The universe will provide." I swallowed, and the involuntary motion was suddenly painful due to a lump in my throat. "Damon's a bad apple having the world's stupidest midlife crisis. Don't let him take your positive outlook from you. The world is full of good people." I could count the ones I knew on one hand, but I was determined to keep her spirits up.

"I don't know …"

"Shut up. Just admit I'm right and we can move on. It's easier that way."

"Okay, you're right. Happy now?"

"I'm thrilled—can't you tell?" I glanced out the window in the back door. "How much have the girls picked up on all this?"

"God only knows what they managed to overhear. Astrid probably gets it more than Sadie."

"Astrid is a sharp cookie."

Isabella let out a soft chuckle. "Like someone else I know."

"Come on," I said. "I was going to make ribs." I pushed open the back door but stopped short. "I didn't know you were coming …"

"No, it's fine! I brought a few things in my cooler. Tofu and some veggies. I'll go get it."

While she retrieved her vegetarian options, I checked the fire and moved the coals to create two cooking areas. I got the marinated and rubbed slabs from the refrigerator and transferred them to the grill, leaving a wide space for Isabella's food. "Behold, the vegetarian zone."

"Everywhere Mom goes is the vegetarian zone," Astrid pointed out as she approached the grill with Braveheart in tow.

Izzy returned with her hands full of tofu packages and an assortment of fresh vegetables. She let them tumble onto the outdoor table.

I glanced at Sadie. "What about you? You want some ribs later?"

Sadie leaned in and sniffed delicately at the smoke. "Maybe."

Isabella smoothed Sadie's hair. Her daughter slipped skinny arms around Isabella's waist.

I retrieved a knife and cutting board for Isabella, then returned to the cabin for a stolen moment of privacy. I had left my phone somewhere in the house before the parade of visitors showed up, and now I cursed the sleek black-on-black color combination of phone and case that made it match so well with my usual outfits. The damn thing was near invisible.

I finally located it balanced precariously on top of the coffee maker. I opened it to the group text that Luella, Pepper, and I shared, and typed a message: *Well, my Sunday's gone to hell.* I composed a summary of Mrs. Millefleur's and Isabella's unannounced arrivals and sent it.

Pepper's reply came back first. *Dang, lady! I was just sitting around in my jammies, bingeing on old episodes of Seinfeld. I can't compete with that kind of drama.*

Luella's message arrived right after Pepper's. *Mrs. Millefleur showed up at your house? You're serious?*

Yes, I wrote. *Can we meet up before work tomorrow morning? I want to talk this over.* We didn't discuss anything magical over devices if we could possibly help it. *Tonight I need to tend to my sister and the kids.*

"Aunt Rose?" Astrid's voice drifted from down the hall.

I shoved the phone in the back of my waistband. "Yes?"

"Mom wanted to know if you had any soy sauce. She didn't bring any."

"I think so." I pulled a half-empty bottle from the refrigerator and held it out.

"Thanks." She took it but didn't turn away to go outside. Instead, she drummed the fingers of her free hand on the kitchen counter. "We're not moving in with you, are we?" Her dark eyes glinted with what looked like more knowledge than Isabella might have guessed.

I concentrated on smoothing my features to give away nothing. "What do you mean?"

She just looked at me.

I knew that look. I used it myself on occasion. "No, you're not moving in with me. Your mom just wanted a little bit of sister time."

Astrid snorted. "Sure she does. I'm not a baby, you know. I'm sixteen. I can drive a car."

"Badly."

Her jaw dropped and her eyes widened in mock outrage.

"I'm kidding, Astrid. Look, you can understand your mom needing a break from the stress, can't you?"

As tough as Astrid pretended to be, she looked like a lost kitten as she considered what I'd said. "Yeah. I guess so." She turned without a word and disappeared out back with the soy sauce.

I released my breath when the back door banged shut. Teenagers.

A glance at my phone revealed that Luella and Pepper had already coordinated an early morning meeting at Rolling Wave Coffee and were awaiting my response to finalize our plans. I tapped out an affirmative and left the phone on the coffee maker before returning to the backyard.

Sadie had found a faded frisbee and was playing catch with Braveheart. Astrid's hair hung over her face like a green and black curtain as she peered at her phone, scrolling and tapping with idle fluency.

My sister poked at the food on the grill.

I pried the tongs out of her hand. "Staring at it won't make it cook faster."

She swished her skirt at me and took a seat at the picnic table next to Astrid. "So who was that lady? She seemed very formal."

"She's the head of the Downtown Merchant Guild. She was trying to get me to join." This was true enough for the moment.

"She came all the way out here to recruit you?"

"It's a very aggressive membership program," I said.

"Wow," said Isabella. "She must have really needed to add a dog trainer to the roster. Or maybe she just loves dogs."

I hid a smile.

Sadie dropped the Frisbee and began to spin in place, slowly at first, causing the hem of her skirt to ripple outward. She whirled until she staggered, then sat down in a heap. Her voice floated faint and soft on the humid afternoon air. "I feel the whole world spinning," she said.

I kept my hands busy at the grill while I surreptitiously observed my sister and the two girls. What would they do if Damon got the house?

Isabella got up, grasped Sadie's hands, and hauled her to her feet. "That's because the whole world *is* spinning, angelface. Take a break before you spin yourself out of an appetite."

Sadie joined her sister on the bench and leaned her head against Astrid's upper arm.

Astrid counterbalanced the additional weight without a protest.

Braveheart, finally tuckered out, sat down to watch squirrels chase each other across the top of the weathered fence.

I envied him. I'd rather have collapsed into the nearest Adirondack chair to watch the squirrels, leaving the drama behind in favor of my cabin, my grill, and my dog. But when it's your family—when their whole world is wobbling on its axis—you marshal your resources.

You fight fire with fire.

3

The sounds of The Cure echoed tinnily from the kitchen where I'd left the phone the night before. I wrapped myself in a blanket and stumbled out of bed to silence the musical alarm before it woke Isabella and the girls. They'd be up soon enough, but I wanted to let them have as much rest as possible.

Braveheart greeted me in the hallway with a sleepy snuffle and a gentle head butt against my knee. I ruffled his ears and opened the back door to let him run around before I left, shutting it quickly to stop the chilly air from seeping in.

Memories from the previous day struck me in quick succession. I winced and tugged the blanket tighter as cold seeped from the floor into my feet. Chilly weather in Florida has a way of sneaking up on you—one day it's ninety degrees, the next day you're shivering under a cold front that steals in overnight.

A hot shower compensated for the coolness. I dried off and selected black slacks and a snug black top. I tossed my favorite beat-up blue jean jacket on the bed next to the outfit.

At the very least, I could make use of my fire magic to take the cold out of the clothing. I contemplated the pieces before me, then tucked my towel tighter to free my hands. I stretched my open hands over the bed and concentrated on imparting warmth to the fabric. I closed my eyes to concentrate. Silver heat trickled through me.

A faint, scorched scent rose to my nostrils. My eyes flew open. A round spot of char appeared on the collar of the jean jacket like someone had used it to put out a cigar. I grimaced and quickly rolled up the jacket to prevent it from actually igniting.

Clearly, I needed more practice.

I dressed in the freshly warmed—and only slightly singed—clothing, and put on my leather ankle boots. With a swipe of dark red lipstick and black eyeliner, I was as ready as I'd ever be.

With Braveheart back in the house and supplied with food and water, I locked up the cabin and hopped in my old truck. Lacking a sleek digital interface and in-car wireless connectivity, I used a cord to plug my phone into the audio jack the old-fashioned way and allowed The Cure to pick up where they'd left off. I half-listened, knowing every song by heart, settling into the familiar rhythm of the music and steadfastly ignoring the twinges of ancient feelings it stirred.

The early morning drive from my cabin to Rolling Wave Coffee took me out of the unincorporated Black Bear Ridge area, through the Sparkle Beach city limits, and across the Intracoastal Waterway bridge as the sun blazed above the eastern horizon.

Rolling Wave Coffee hung on as an extension of the Eventide, one of the old-school, family-run beachside motels. In the parking lot, I pushed the truck door open against a stiff sea breeze and had to dodge as the wind tried to slam the door shut for me. I hastened to the entrance and pulled open the door to the sound of the coffee grinder in action. I spotted Luella at a couch in the back, and I waved before stepping up to the wooden counter to place my order—double shot espresso. I carried my cup to the far couch and dropped into the deep cushions.

"Happy Monday," said Luella.

I snorted into my cup.

Luella wrapped her fingers around a mug of milk-filled concoction topped with cinnamon. "Drink up. Surely the caffeine will help."

I tossed back the bitter liquid. "Nothing's that strong. I'm not sure what would help at this point."

A voice carried from across the shop. "What's up, witches?" Pepper pointed finger guns at us before gesturing toward the menu board. "I'm just gonna get something." She stepped up to the counter and had an animated discussion with the clerk, who sprang into action and began assembling Pepper's order.

Pepper marched over with her own mug of drip coffee and a tray full of pastries. "I got enough to share." She bit into an enormous bear claw, showering her khakis with crumbs of pastry and sugar.

"Thanks, Pepper." I snagged a chocolate croissant and took a bite.

Luella's hand hovered over a muffin, a donut, and a cinnamon bun like a UFO deciding where to land. "Why not?" she said philosophically as she grabbed the oversized bun.

Pepper applauded her choice and nearly smashed her bearclaw in the process. "Oops!" She grinned.

I trailed the tip of the croissant in the dregs of espresso. "You seem in a good mood."

"Who, me?" Pepper laughed and set down her pastry. "I guess I am."

I raised my eyebrows.

She nodded, as if to emphasize the point. "Pete finally arranged to have someone other than me cover the office when they're short."

Luella and I exchanged a look. Pepper referred to her husband as "Pete" when she was pleased, "Peter" when she was not.

"Really? Permanently?" said Luella.

"Permanently," said Pepper. "No more triple-duty for me. Now all I have on my plate is the kids and my job at Suntan Queen."

"Still a lot," I said.

"But better than having the kids, Suntan Queen, and Pete's office to take care of," added Luella.

"How'd you get through to him?" I asked.

Pepper set down her bearclaw, her face scrunched in thought. "I don't know. Maybe I picked something up from hanging around Queenie so much. That lady may call everyone 'darling,' but she's a force of nature."

Luella cleared her throat. "Speaking of forces of nature, what are we going to do about Mrs. Millefleur?" She paused, as if she was about to address a delicate matter. "You don't *want* to learn from her, do you?"

I tilted my head as I considered. I didn't—did I? Another uncomfortable feeling to shove down with the rest. "I wish I could stop her from showing up at my house. I mean, not that I want to see her anywhere, but with Isabella and the girls staying with me ..."

"It's hard to hide a couple of witches setting things on fire," said Pepper.

Luella said nothing, but leaned back and settled her gaze on me.

"Don't look at me like that, Luella."

"You didn't actually answer my question," she replied.

"You took a house from her." I regretted the words as soon as they left my lips. I hung my head. "I'm sorry. I don't know what's gotten into me. I shouldn't have made a crack about your house—"

She sipped her coffee peaceably. "No harm done."

I gave her a grateful look. "It's just that you have your mama, and Pepper has Queenie"—Mrs. Millefleur's words echoed in my mind as I realized I was repeating them—"and I'm blundering along in the dark. Ironic, really. For a fire witch."

"Plus you have three houseguests," said Pepper. "And a soon-to-be ex-brother-in-law who needs to be taken out."

"Exactly. It couldn't possibly get any more complicated."

"Maybe you should talk to Mrs. Millefleur. See what she wants," said Luella.

I scoffed. "No one really knows what she wants. And she doesn't seem to be into handing out explanations. We still don't know why she pulled that stunt at the lighthouse—only that she said something was coming."

The sound of the coffee grinder punctuated the silence.

Pepper glanced at her water-resistant watch. "I better get a to-go bag."

I noticed her hair was dry. "Did you surf this morning, Pepper?"

"Nah. Queenie and I are planning to take an extended lunch break today." A pleased look stole over her face. She stood up. "Strictly business."

Luella chuckled. "Strictly water-witchy business," she said as Pepper walked away.

I smiled, but couldn't suppress a pang of envy. I hoped Luella didn't notice.

She didn't—she had looked away from Pepper to gaze at her phone.

"Good news?"

"Raphael's in the garden again." She displayed the screen, which showed a picture of her boyfriend, Raphael, kneeling in a heap of dirt and surrounded by plants. "His new obsession."

I dutifully admired the photo. Raphael's enthusiastic nature meshed well with Luella's appreciation for the simple joys of life, and I felt satisfied to see her so content. "What's Zephyr up to?"

"She was in the garden when I left—blowing the empty plastic pots around. Why? Did you want to see her?"

"Am I that transparent?"

Luella's eyes sparkled. "We've got a few minutes before we have to get to Suntan Queen."

Pepper returned, paper bag in hand. "Got a few minutes for what?"

Luella tossed the remaining pastries in the bag. "Come on." She led the way out the door and down the wooden boardwalk. The wind freed a gray-striped lock of hair from her braid.

Pepper and I followed. We all stopped at the stairs and pulled off our shoes.

"Zephyr!" called Luella as she bounded down the last few steps of the stairs and onto the sandy beach.

Luella's magical white-and-silver flying dog appeared in an instant. She blew across the dunes, tossing sand in her wake. She raced across the wide expanse of beach and dashed through the crashing whitecaps.

Pepper whooped and gave chase. She ran to the water's edge and made a sweeping motion with her free hand that blasted a cascade of water in Zephyr's direction.

Luella pressed her lips together in a look of concentration. A draft of wind tumbled an incoming wave at Pepper, forcing her to dance backward to avoid getting soaked in cold water.

That gave me an idea—and an opportunity to practice my warming magic. "Come here," I said to Luella and Pepper. "Get your feet in the water."

"But it's cold!" said Pepper.

"Trust me."

They inched closer. Zephyr joined them, her tail wagging as she watched the waves.

The next wave gathered itself in the distance. I threaded a string of fire magic outward, tracing the roiling lines of the wave like silver Christmas lights on a hedge—a moving, tumbling, churning hedge. I held the flames like a leash, preserving the magical fire against the water, until the wave reached its greatest height. I released the heat into the wave as it crashed upon the shore. The toppled wave slid across the sand and covered our feet with water as warm as a freshly drawn bath.

Luella and Pepper clapped and cheered.

I smiled to myself as I looked out to sea. Perhaps I didn't need Mrs. Millefleur after all.

4

The Suntan Queen factory groaned to life like a mechanical beast as my coworkers and I set the machinery in motion. With a full crew on the floor, we'd be able to knock out the day's production run in a few hours.

The sunscreen ingredients were heated and mixed in shiny steel tanks. The white liquid shot into bottles which were quickly replaced with empties. The full bottles clicked into place under robotic clamps that crimped the top end while a printer applied the lot and expiration date. Once sealed, they rolled down a chute into plastic bins for later packing.

Years of experience meant I did less work directly on the production line, more supervising and troubleshooting—but it still required a decent level of focus. Coconut-scented air filled my lungs as I took a deep breath to clear my mind. I snagged several bottles of sunscreen fresh off the conveyor

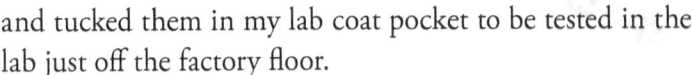

and tucked them in my lab coat pocket to be tested in the lab just off the factory floor.

The heavy lab door muffled the clicks, whirrs, and thumps of production. Alone in the lab, I set my safety goggles aside and retrieved a tray of testing materials. A batch of sunscreen didn't leave the factory without going through quality control first. You couldn't just ship it out and hope for the best—you had to put it to the test to make sure it performed as promised.

I completed the sequence of testing on automatic pilot, humming one of the songs that had played in the truck earlier in the morning.

The rest of the shift passed in a blur of activity. By the time I'd hung up my white coat and safety goggles in my locker, a jittery feeling had overtaken me. I looked around for Pepper, but she'd already left for her lunchtime surfing escapade. Luella was out on a photo shoot with her intern, London. I pulled out my phone to text them, but all such thoughts flew out of my head when I opened a message from my sister: *Could you possibly stop by my house on your way home and pick up a few warmer things for the girls? I didn't anticipate this cold front coming in.*

An unpleasant task, certainly—but I had a key, and I had the advantage of not being married to the ass who currently shared the house. Perhaps he would provoke me, and then I could set his hair on fire. I smiled, stuffed the phone in my pocket, and headed out to my truck.

I drove without consciously paying attention to where I was going, lost in the fantasy of burning Damon to a crisp and letting a herd of hippos trample the ashes. I blew past the turnoff to my cabin and stayed on the old highway through Black Bear Ridge to the border of the tiny college town on the other side of the forest from Sparkle Beach. At the entrance to Izzy's neighborhood, I turned in, followed the curve to Izzy's street, and eased the truck into the driveway of her bungalow-style house.

A half-dozen windchimes made from recycled bottles greeted me with bell-like sounds. I followed the footpath past an assortment of rusting folk art sculptures to the front door. Wildflowers in Izzy's native plant garden bobbed in the breeze—she'd been in the process of xeriscaping the front yard.

I knocked, intending to open the door regardless of whether I got a response, but I didn't even have time to put the key in the lock before Damon opened the door.

He observed me without a greeting, wearing linen drawstring pants and a nubby sweater, his ponytail pulled slightly askew. He leaned against the doorframe with an unwelcoming grunt. "Did your sister send you?"

Anger bubbled through me like champagne. I didn't bother with a smile; instead, I leveled what I hoped was a blistering glare. *Give me a reason, Damon.* "The girls need some stuff."

"Whatever. Just be quick about it." He stepped aside so I had barely enough room to squeeze past.

"Thanks," I said, allowing the sarcasm to drip freely. Without the presence of my sister and nieces, the house seemed darker, mustier, less lively. The colorful hand-dyed fabric hangings on the wall looked forlorn rather than cheerful. I patted a large wooden sculpture of frogs as I passed it—Izzy's favorite treasure—but even the frogs seemed to frown.

Damon crossed his arms. "Why don't you pack it all in your truck at one go? That way you won't need to come back."

That did it. I whirled on him. "You pathetic excuse for a human being. How dare you try to chase my sister and your children out of their home?"

He shrugged. "Her choice. She left."

"You were so awful to be around, you *made* her leave."

"I didn't *make* her do anything."

Silver flames boiled over my hands. Thank God he couldn't see them. Setting his pant leg on fire sounded like a good idea, but attacking him face-to-face might end with me in jail, even if the evidence was slim. Could I hypnotize him? I couldn't think of anything I could get him to go along with off the top of my head, and I couldn't stop picturing flames crawling up his pants.

I opened my mouth to issue a scathing retort but snapped it shut at an unfamiliar noise: the musical sound of a cat's meow.

I blinked. Izzy didn't have any pets.

Had Damon gotten one? That didn't seem like his style.

I leaned to the right, enough to see around Damon's shoulder, and caught sight of a golden-eyed black cat approaching on silent paws. I murmured the Shakespeare line that popped into my head: "'The cat will mew, and the dog will have his day.'"

Damon, following my gaze, glanced over his shoulder with annoyance. "What?"

I didn't take my eyes off the cat as I repeated my words. "I said, 'The cat will mew, and the dog will have its day.' Hamlet."

"What the hell are you babbling about?"

The black cat wound around Damon's ankles, then sat, twitching its tail. Damon didn't notice a thing. With a soft pop, the tip of the cat's tail ignited with a silver glow that coalesced into a steady argent flame.

I gasped, and quickly covered my mouth with my hand. *That is not Damon's cat. He doesn't even see it.*

He rolled his eyes. "Look, Rose, I don't know what your deal is, but I think you should go."

The cat meowed, and flicked its tail at Damon's pant leg.

I suppressed a laugh. *Oh, no. Bad kitty!*

"Is this funny to you?"

With that, the cat delicately rested its tail on Damon's foot and touched the flaming tip of its tail to the hem of Damon's pants.

The pants smoldered, then ignited.

I smoothed my facial expression while doing my best to ignore the light wisp of smoke curling upward. "Is what funny?"

"You're both crazy—" He broke off mid-sentence and sniffed. Then he looked down and screamed. He stumbled sideways, shaking his leg like an idiot, adding oxygen to the fire. "Help!"

"Stop, drop, and roll, stupid!" I gave him a mighty shove and knocked him to the floor.

The black cat darted out of the way but continued to watch, its golden eyes shining with interest.

I seized a heavy pillow with big tassels and proceeded to beat Damon with it as hard as I could. To put out the fire, of course.

"Ow!" He curled into a ball on the floor.

"Shut up—I'm saving you." The flames died, but I hit him a few more times for good measure. Needless to say, it felt great.

He grabbed the pillow and a brief tug-of-war ensued.

I let go just as he was pulling himself up, which threw him off-balance enough to send him sprawling on the floor again.

He clutched the pillow like it was a teddy bear. "What happened to my pants?" His bewildered tone might have won my sympathy if I didn't hate his guts.

I stepped over him and closed the distance between myself and the cat. Its gaze met mine. I nodded, as one professional to another. *Good kitty.* With my back to Damon, I patted my thigh.

The cat ran to me, its burbling meow music to my ears.

A fire cat! I couldn't wait to tell Luella and Pepper, but first I had to do what I'd come for. I left Damon on the floor and retreated down the hall with the cat trailing behind me. In the privacy of Astrid's room, I knelt and caressed my new kitty friend. Its fur felt silky like a normal cat, but with radiant heat like an open oven door. "Who's the baddest good kitty in the world?"

The cat rolled on its back and stretched luxuriously, batting its black paws in the air.

I stood and began sorting through clothes. "We'll have to come up with a good name for you." The line from *Hamlet* came back to mind. "Not Hamlet. Spoiler alert—he dies." I chuckled to myself. "How about Horatio? For a true and faithful friend."

Horatio gave me the look of a king accepting his royal tribute.

"That was a fine trick you pulled out there, by the way." I retrieved a handful of clothing from a drawer and started a pile on the bed.

Horatio jumped onto the bed and picked his way across the rumpled covers. He curled up in the pile and began washing his paws.

"Trust a cat to do whatever it wants, and to hell with the consequences." I started another pile next to Horatio. "I wonder if you'll come when I call, like Zephyr does?"

The cat appeared to be studiously ignoring me, using body language to indicate the answer: *If I feel like it.*

"I'm going to get Sadie's stuff." I left Astrid's room and crossed the hall. Judging by the noise coming from down the hall, Damon had peeled himself off the floor and was banging things around in the kitchen. In Sadie's room, my gaze went first to the open closet, in which hung an assortment of pieces much smaller than Astrid's.

A light burst in my peripheral vision like a silvery camera flash. I turned, expecting to find a burned-out lightbulb in the lamp on the bedside table.

Instead, I found Horatio sitting pretty on Sadie's pillow. He looked utterly pleased with his feat of apparition.

"You could have just walked across the hall, you know." I gathered an armful of Sadie's things and carried them back to the piles in Astrid's room.

Horatio deigned to follow me on foot.

In Astrid's room, I stuffed the collected items into an overturned laundry basket I found on the floor, then dusted my hands. "Ready, Horatio?"

We faced each other, fire witch to fire cat. His golden eyes seemed infinitely deep. I couldn't tell if he was looking into my soul—or if he *was* my soul.

With a pop and a flash, he disappeared.

A warmth draped over my shoulders. Horatio had settled himself in place like a living neck warmer, at the same time weighing nothing and everything.

I reached up and scratched his kitty head. "Make yourself at home, you fiery little beastie."

His answering purr rumbled through my shoulders.

I grabbed the overstuffed laundry basket with both hands and hauled it down the hallway.

"Are you leaving?" Damon called. He sauntered out of the kitchen holding a mug of something in his hands.

"Yeah, I'm leaving." *Jerk.* The basket tired my arms, but even setting it down for a moment was too long to linger in Damon's presence. Not to mention the fact that he reeked of burn cream.

He smirked. "Bye, then."

His arrogant expression crystallized my feelings into diamond-hard resolve. I'd get him out of my sister's house if it killed me. I concentrated on the liquid in his mug, hoping I could heat it long-distance enough to burn his mouth when he drank.

The liquid steamed—and then the body of the mug exploded, spraying hot liquid and shards all over Damon, who shrieked, then stared in shock at the detached mug handle in his hand.

Oops. Lost a little control there. No regrets; he deserved it. I tilted my head and swept him with a look of contempt. "Don't worry. I'll be back." With that, I turned on my heel and strode out the door.

5

Braveheart met me at the door of the cabin. He took one look at Horatio and barked in sharp surprise, then turned in a rapid circle and sat, flummoxed by the golden-eyed black cat on my shoulders.

I already knew Braveheart could see magic that humans didn't—he'd been instant best friends with Luella's magical dog, Zephyr—but it was still amusing to watch his reaction.

Horatio jumped down from my shoulder and sauntered toward Braveheart.

Braveheart crouched to Horatio's eye level.

The cat paused, his fire-tipped tail waving in a serpentine manner.

I watched them, alert for signs of trouble. "Come on, guys, we're all friends here."

Braveheart inched closer. He gave Horatio a mighty sniff.

Horatio regarded the dog with something between tolerance and pity. He padded away down the hallway.

Braveheart scrambled to a standing position and let out a sneeze, then trotted companionably behind the cat. His nails clicked on the hard floors.

I followed them, opened the back door, and shooed them into the backyard. "Don't light the pine straw on fire," I said. After shutting the door, I returned to the living room to sort the girls' clothing and shoes. I placed the sorted stacks in the guest bedroom.

I changed into my comfy pants and stretched out on the couch with my feet propped up. I opened the group text with Luella and Pepper and added a new message: *Guess what? I have a new friend.*

Pepper's reply appeared. *Is he tall, dark, and handsome?* Then a pause. *Is he married?*

Typical Pepper. She was a hopeless romantic who wanted to see everyone married. *No to the first, yes to the second and third, and I'm not sure he believes in the institution of marriage*, I wrote.

You can make it work, said Pepper.

Also, he's a cat, I added—with a few cat emojis for good measure.

Luella chimed in, cautiously skirting the limits of what we felt comfortable discussing via text: *Would this happen to be a special kind of cat?*

Very special, I replied. *You want to meet him?*

A blizzard of affirmative words and emojis arrived.

I signed off with a promise to get together as soon as I had a free moment safe from prying eyes. The crunch of gravel and the clatter of keys at the front door signaled the arrival of Izzy, Astrid, and Sadie. I sat up and abandoned my phone just in time for the three of them to bustle through the door.

"Did you get the stuff?" said Izzy. She lugged her rolling file crate into a corner and retracted the handle.

"I did."

"And?" Her eyebrows lifted in an unspoken question: *Did Damon give you a hard time?*

I let my gaze flick meaningfully to the girls and back to Izzy.

"Right," said Izzy. "We'll talk in a minute. Girls, do you have homework?"

"I'm hungry," said Sadie.

"I'll do mine later." Astrid attempted to sidle down the hallway.

"No, you won't. Have a snack, and get your sister something, too. Then get your work done."

Thwarted in her escape, Astrid sighed and tousled Sadie's hair. "Come on, short stuff."

"Okay, big stuff."

They dropped their backpacks and retreated to the kitchen.

Izzy made eye contact and jerked her head in the direction of the backyard.

I stood and followed her outside.

Braveheart was still dashing around the sandy backyard. Horatio had curled up on the lid of the grill, leaving the exertion to the dog.

Izzy settled at the picnic table. "So?"

I slid onto the bench facing her. "It went about like you would imagine." How could I explain the pants-on-fire and the exploding coffee cup? I hadn't shared the secret of my magical powers with anyone non-magical yet—but with the arrival of Horatio, I was dying to tell Izzy everything. "Except for a couple of weird incidents, that is." I related the story without sharing my part in it, framing the strange happenings as the universe taking its revenge.

It worked. Izzy doubled over in peals of laughter.

A clammy wet blanket of guilt landed on my warm glow of satisfaction. I hated keeping something this important, this life-changing, from Izzy.

Braveheart galumphed over to the table and laid his head on Izzy's knee.

She patted his head absentmindedly. "Exploding coffee cups and spontaneous combustion … now if only the house itself would attack him, maybe he'd abandon it."

I did a double take. My peace-loving sister had more ferocity than I'd expected. "Maybe he would," I mused. My gaze strayed to Horatio, who remained curled up on top of the grill.

"I'm being silly," she said with a wistful air. "I have to face this with cold, practical facts. My position as an adjunct professor is never going to pay the bills as a single mom. My house may not even be mine anymore. And now I've imposed on my own sister just because—"

"You're no imposition."

Izzy gave a wan smile. "Of course not."

"No, Isabella, listen to me. You needed a break to clear your head. We're family. This is what we do for each other." I reached across the table and gripped her hands in mine.

They were cold, so I chafed them. "You remember how it was after Dad left—you, me, and Mom, against the world?"

"I remember."

"We made it, didn't we? You got through college. I made enough working at Suntan Queen to save up for a down payment on the cabin. We did all the things Mom dreamed we would do."

Isabella squeezed my hands. "I miss Mom."

Those three words were enough to snap me in half, but I couldn't let it show. I had to be the strong one, for Izzy's sake. "I miss her, too."

In the silence that followed, a bright silver flash caused stars to dance across my vision. Horatio had disappeared from the top of the grill only to reappear on the table. He settled himself over our hands, and his warmth radiated through my fingers.

Tears pricked at my eyes. This secret was too much. "Izzy, I—"

The back door flew open. Horatio jumped into my lap.

"Mom! Guess what!" Sadie leaped down the steps and crossed the backyard at a run, her little cowgirl boots flying under her prairie skirt. "There's a circus coming to Sparkle Beach! Can we go, Mom, please? With sprinkles on top?"

Astrid followed her younger sister outside at a more leisurely pace. "Check it out." She turned her phone around and displayed a social media post featuring an aerialist dangling from swaths of fabric.

Izzy leaned in for a closer look. She read the profile name aloud: "Circus Aetherium."

"Let me see that." I held out my hand for the phone. Spotlights illuminated the aerialist with a wash of colors. The inky background made it look like she was floating in space.

Sadie bounced up and down. "And they have fire dancers!"

Horatio cautiously poked his head over my arm as I scrolled through the profile on Astrid's phone. The next sequence of photos showcased a dancer with a hoop of flames suspended around her bare midriff. "Don't try this at home, kids," I muttered. I handed the phone back to Astrid.

"How much are tickets?" asked Izzy.

The girls looked at each other and shrugged.

Circus tickets, I knew, would not be on anyone's list of necessities. Under normal circumstances, Izzy would have cheerfully treated the girls to a show like the Circus Aetherium without a second thought. I could tell from the look on my sister's face that her worries revolved around the thought of money—and how there wouldn't be enough of it, thanks to the impending divorce, Izzy's small salary, and Damon's selfish claim on the house. Maybe the tickets weren't important in the scheme of things, but I was loath to lose even this small battle. Izzy was clearly looking for a way to let the girls down easy. I caught her gaze and lifted my chin, a signal to hold off on saying no.

She raised her eyebrows, but went along. "We'll look into it."

Horatio purred on my lap like a very small lawnmower.

As his warmth stole over me, I found myself inhaling the winter air with greater freedom. I closed my eyes and listened to the sound of the wind whistling through the pine branches. The scent of water twined with the sharp tang of pine sap. Somewhere, deeper in the forest, hidden springs bubbled from beneath the earth.

But what did the serenity of nature matter, if I felt helpless to fix the world as it needed to be fixed?

Something would have to be done.

Izzy's voice pierced my meditation. "Rose?"

I opened my eyes.

"You all right?"

Hidden under the table, my fingers sank into Horatio's fur. "I'm all right. I think I'll go inside for a bit." I directed my next thought at Horatio: *Come on, kitty. We have work to do.*

He followed me into the house.

I retrieved my phone and sent Luella a message: *Are you and your mom still picking oranges after work tomorrow? Would you mind if I tagged along? There's some things I'd like to discuss.*

The elements of nature didn't work alone, and neither could I.

6

The small orange grove would never have been featured on a postcard. It appeared the owners had seen fit to let it fall into a state of benign neglect. Whenever the scraggly trees managed to produce a few oranges, they set up a folding table and allowed visitors to pick fruit and pay by the basket.

After parking my truck on the side of the dirt lane, I approached the table to collect a few baskets. Under the guise of smoothing my hair, I patted Horatio, who rode on his favorite perch—my shoulders.

The nearby orange-laden branches bobbed in a sudden wind.

Luella and her mother stood a short distance into the grove, in between two rows of orange trees. They spotted me and waved. Zephyr's white-and-silver coat shone in the sun as she darted out from under a tree to join them.

I returned the wave and walked over.

Luella pressed her hands to her cheeks when she caught sight of Horatio. "Oh, my goodness! Rose! He's beautiful."

I smiled. "Thank you for letting us crash your fruit-picking spree."

Mama leaned in for a closer look at the cat. "Hey there, you little devil."

Luella brandished her baskets. "Shall we go further in?"

We strolled deeper into the grove without speaking.

When Mama judged that we'd gone far enough, she raised her hand to signal a halt. "Let me get a good look at this critter."

I stepped close to Mama, who peered at Horatio for a long moment.

She gave him an indulgent scratch behind his ears, and he submitted to her touch with a rumbly purr. "He seems to like riding around up there like a little prince."

In true catlike fashion, Horatio immediately hopped down—as if to say *I do what I want, when I want.* He sprinted away into the trees with Zephyr bounding along behind.

Luella shaded her eyes from the bright sun as she watched them go. "Think they'll get into any trouble?"

"An air dog and a fire cat?" I said. "What could possibly go wrong?"

Mama snorted.

I retold the story of Horatio's appearance while we picked oranges. I added in all the parts I'd left out of the story when I told it to Izzy. As I came to the end of the tale, my hand closed around a brightly colored orange. I pulled hard to snap the stem—too hard. The orange flew out of my grasp, bounced off Luella's shoulder, and landed on her mother's foot.

"Ow," said Mama. "Watch where you're throwing those things."

Whoever came up with the expression "killing two birds with one stone" probably wouldn't have predicted the variation of hitting two witches with one orange. "Sorry." I retrieved the orange from where it had rolled under another tree, and added it to the basket.

"Your sister's husband sounds like a real piece of work," said Luella.

"He is, indeed."

Mama's expression grew thoughtful. "I suspect you have more in mind for him than just burnt pants and exploding cups."

"I wish. But I don't know what would actually help my sister." I threw down an orange with more force than was strictly necessary. "Part of me wants to solve everything for everyone. Part of me wants to run away and join the circus."

Luella and her mother exchanged a look.

"What?" I said.

"Funny you should mention that." Mama picked up three oranges and juggled them expertly. The oranges trailed silver sparkles as they flew through the air.

"You're using your magic to help you juggle oranges?"

"'Course I am, girl." Mama caught the oranges—one, two, three—in quick succession. "Use it or lose it, I always say. Never know what it'll come in handy for till you try."

I touched an orange on a nearby branch, then released it. It was too green. "I don't see how I can use my magic to solve any of this. Maybe if I knew more. Maybe if I…"

"Maybe if you what?" said Mama.

Luella held two oranges, one in each hand. The pose made her resemble a blind justice of citrus. She gave me an encouraging gesture with the fruit.

I hesitated. "Maybe if I took Mrs. Millefleur up on her offer."

Luella's gaze shot to her mother.

Mama didn't react, at first. She kept rummaging in the branches.

"It's probably a bad idea," I added.

"Hilda Millefleur," said Mama, speaking into the tree rather than making eye contact with me, "is a sneaky old broad with more secrets than gray hairs." She faced me. "I don't believe in forgive and forget. I haven't forgiven and I won't forget the danger she put Luella in, but—"

"Mama—" Luella interrupted.

"Hush, child. I ain't finished. *But* the one thing I know is she doesn't do anything without a damn good reason. It may not be my reason, or your reason, but there's *always* a reason."

"Otherwise Mama would have shot her already," added Luella, in a half-joking tone.

"I ain't stupid enough to use a gun," said Mama. "That's how you get caught."

It seemed like a good time to change the subject. "Speaking of secrets—Luella told me your late husband knew about your magic."

Mama nodded. "He did. I told him years into our marriage, when I was sure I could trust him."

I laughed. "Didn't you trust him when you married him?"

"There's trust—and then there's *trust*. You don't go sharing secrets like that until you've been through some stuff." Mama discarded an orange that had been nibbled on by some creature. "You got someone in mind you wanna tell?"

"Her sister," said Luella.

"Don't get me started on siblings," said Mama. "Can't live with 'em, can't shoot 'em. No offense," she added.

"None taken." I tossed an orange from hand to hand. "Isabella and I have definitely been through some stuff."

Mama eyed me. "It's your call. Ain't none of us going to tell you what to do with family. Family's family, and that's all there is to it." She gripped an orange and held it right up to my face. "You want to train with Hilda Millefleur? Train with Hilda Millefleur. But you keep one eye on the ball at all times, you hear me?" She dropped the orange in the basket with a decisive *thump*.

Horatio and Zephyr returned from wherever they'd gone. Zephyr nipped playfully at the flame on Horatio's tail, and earned a lightning-fast paw in the face. The hit didn't faze Zephyr. She flopped on the grass in good humor, her tail swishing from side to side.

Horatio placed a paw on one of the fallen oranges, leaving a black paw-shaped brand on the skin.

I sniffed, and caught the acrid odor of burning citrus. "Horatio, behave."

He curled up with regal grace and watched us finish filling the baskets.

When the baskets couldn't hold one single orange more, we carried our haul to the table. I pulled cash from my pocket and handed it over. With two full baskets, there would be enough oranges to last Izzy, the girls, and me for days. No matter what else was going on, at least no one in our household would lack vitamin C.

I dropped off my baskets in the truck. Horatio caught a ride on my shoulders and Zephyr bounded alongside as I walked Luella and Mama to Luella's car. I hugged them goodbye, and had already turned away to go back to my truck, when a thought occurred to me. "Mama—where's your bird?"

"Midnight?" said Luella.

"I already told you—I ain't calling him that. He's just Crow." She gestured vaguely. "He's around."

"Can I ask you something?"

"Shoot."

"Why do some of us have these magical animals, and some of us don't?"

Mama leaned against the car and crossed her arms. "We all have them. Some witches just haven't found theirs yet, and others, well … they hide theirs."

My eyebrows shot up. "Hide them? Why?"

"So they can't be spotted by another witch."

"But you don't hide yours—"

"I ain't afraid of nobody. If some witch wants to mess with me, they can come get me."

"Is that a real risk?"

"Life's a real risk." With those words, a blue-black crow swooped from nowhere and landed on her shoulder.

7

The next day, I completed my Suntan Queen shift with one eye on the clock. Heavy gray clouds rolled in from the west and loomed in my rearview mirror as I turned out of the parking lot after work. Horatio curled up comfortably on the passenger seat of the truck, and seemed content to lash his fire-tipped tail occasionally in time with the music.

My fingers tightened around the steering wheel. I wasn't going to wait for Hilda Millefleur to show up at my cabin again. If she liked unannounced arrivals so much, I'd give her one of my own. I knew where to find her, after all: Millefleur Properties, conveniently located downtown and only a few blocks from Suntan Queen. I pressed the gas pedal and came a little too close to the downtown speed limits.

Horatio lifted his head and made an inquisitive noise.

"Don't worry, Horatio. I have it all under control. What could go wrong?" I glanced at his golden eyes, which had the mesmeric quality of a crackling fire. "Never mind. Don't answer that."

Millefleur Properties occupied an old yellow brick building at the south end of River Street. I squeezed the truck into the parking space next to Mrs. Millefleur's white Town Car, which had its own reserved space. "Come on, kitty. Let's get witchy."

Horatio set his claws into the fabric of the seat and had a luxurious stretch.

I got out and waited with the door open, unsure if he would follow.

With a flash and a pop, he disappeared from the seat and reappeared on my shoulders.

At least he kept out the chill.

I crossed the sidewalk and pulled open the glass door. It swung wide, accompanied by the jangle of bells.

An older woman with purple-gray hair sat at the reception desk. She blinked at me through purple-tinted lenses. "Well, hello, young lady. What can I do for you?"

I raised an eyebrow at *young lady*. "Is Mrs. Millefleur around?"

"She's out right now."

"But I saw her car outside …" I looked over my shoulder, through the glass door, as if I had somehow imagined parking next to the Town Car.

"She probably snuck out the back and walked. You can ask Oliver, if you want."

"Oliver?"

"Her chauffeur." She pronounced the French word by stretching it out like bubble gum. "He's a nice dude," she added. "He won't mind."

"Good to know." Better than the alternative, anyway. I glanced at her coffee mug, which read *Gladys's Coffee: Do Not Touch on Pain of Death.* "Thanks—Gladys."

"You're welcome, dear."

I retreated to the sidewalk and stood irresolute under the darkening sky, pretending to check my phone. A stealthy glance at the Town Car confirmed the silhouette of a man in the driver's seat. What would my friends do in this situation? Luella would pour on the Southern charm. Pepper would probably pretend to fall off the sidewalk, as a conversation starter.

I, on the other hand, had neither Southern charm nor the inclination to pull off a pratfall. It would have to be my own way.

Horatio flexed his claw into my shoulder, giving me something between an affectionate squeeze and a puncture wound.

Spurred—literally—I strode to the white Town Car and rapped on the driver's window.

It rolled down with a hum to reveal a man in a black suit and a white shirt.

His gaze met mine with dry amusement. "Are you lost?" He had a real British accent, complete with crisp pronunciation and something of a worldly tone.

I blinked. His accent shouldn't have thrown me, but it did. I was too busy being surprised to even be insulted that he had basically just called me a tourist. "No, I'm not lost. I'm looking for your employer."

"Ah, the elusive Mrs. Millefleur. She occupies this very office." He gestured to the building in front of us. "Might I suggest you speak to the secretary inside?"

"I already did. Gladys said to ask you." I leaned down to get a better look at him, and the inside of the car. A stack of books filled the passenger seat. "She described you as a 'nice dude.'"

"Did she?" His gaze shifted to the front of the building, then back to me. "I suppose I am—nice, that is. In the classic sense of the word."

I folded my arms. "I know what 'nice' means. In the classic and the modern sense." No one, not even British men in black suits, could out-vocabulary me.

His lips formed the ghost of a smile. "I have no doubt that you do." He glanced at my bicep, as if he could somehow see the rose and fire tattoo underneath my sleeve.

Horatio gave a light shiver on my shoulders.

I resisted the urge to settle him with a comforting pat. "Can you take me to her?"

"To whom?"

"Who do you think?"

He drummed his fingers on the steering wheel with a smart *rat-a-tat-tat*. "I'm afraid not."

"Why not?"

"Because—I'm sorry, what was your name again?"

I hadn't given it in the first place. "Rose."

"Because, Rose"—he paused—"if she's not in the office, and she's not in this car, then she snuck out the back and didn't tell me where she was going. Very frustrating." He looked genuinely perturbed.

"On foot?"

"Presumably."

Horatio jumped down from my shoulders, twitched his fire-tipped tail, and began walking north on the sidewalk.

Perhaps the cat knew something I didn't. I turned to follow Horatio, then stopped and turned back to the chauffeur. In my eagerness to follow Horatio, I'd nearly wandered off without a word of explanation. "Perhaps I'll find her on River Street. Thank you for your help," I added, out of politeness.

He swiftly opened the door and alighted on the pavement. "I could help you look for her. I know her haunts, as it were."

"There's no need."

"Please, allow me to assist." He closed the door and stepped up onto the sidewalk, revealing the full length of his well-cut black suit. He settled a black chauffeur's cap over neatly combed hair and regarded me with steady intensity.

On second thought, surely I had a better chance of tracking down Mrs. Millefleur if I had her rather good-looking chauffeur *and* a magical cat helping me. "Fine. Let's go."

He nodded once. "As you wish." The deferential words contrasted with the spark in his eyes.

I followed Horatio, who set a leisurely pace, and Oliver walked alongside me. "How long have you worked for Mrs. Millefleur?" I asked.

"Several years now."

"Did she always have a chauffeur?"

"Is that pertinent?"

I gave him a look.

He relented. "Not to my knowledge."

"Why would she go to the trouble of having a chauffeur if she was going to wander off on foot?"

"Are you insinuating that I'm trouble?"

"'Double, double, toil and trouble,'" I said, wondering why I'd agreed to let this person tag along on my search.

He stopped in the middle of the sidewalk. "Quoting Macbeth? Are you a Shakespeare fan?"

"No," I lied, and kept walking.

He hurried to catch up. "What's your favorite play?"

"I don't have one." Also a lie.

Oliver kept talking as if I had confided my favorite. "Mine is *The Winter's Tale*."

I caught myself as I was about to launch into a discussion of the relative merits of Shakespeare's plays. Instead, I made a noncommittal noise.

"It's quite chilly today; perhaps you would like a coffee? Or tea? There's a cafe around the corner—"

"I thought we were looking for Mrs. Millefleur."

"Of course we are. We can get it to go."

He sounded so reasonable, and the idea so inviting, that the vision of a double espresso nearly derailed my footsteps. What was wrong with me? Why couldn't I focus? It was all the fault of this ridiculous Shakespeare-loving chauffeur who wouldn't stop being British and charming. "To go," I said, with as much censure as possible.

"Splendid." He rubbed his hands together, presumably in a mixture of delight and an attempt to ward off the chill.

Horatio looked back at us.

Oliver veered away toward the coffee shop, but stopped when I didn't follow him.

"I'll be right there. Just have to tie my shoelace." I slid my right boot out of view behind my left ankle so he couldn't confirm that the shoelace in question was very much tied.

He hesitated. "Are you sure?"

I nodded. "I'll have a double shot of espresso, please, if you'd like to order."

He inclined his head to me, like a small version of a bow, before disappearing into the shop.

I shook my head. Oliver was unlike any Sparkle Beach man I'd ever encountered. I caught up to Horatio and knelt beside him, then fiddled with my shoelace as I spoke to the cat quietly. "Am I right in thinking you're able to sense where Mrs. Millefleur is?"

Horatio purred and bumped my knee with his head.

"I'll take that as a yes. Let me get this coffee business out of the way and I'll be right with you." I stood.

The cat sat on his haunches and began grooming himself as if the whole escapade was his idea.

Oliver emerged from the coffee shop with a pair of to-go cups.

I approached him and took the proffered cup, which steamed into the winter air as a handful of raindrops spattered the sidewalk. I tossed back the espresso and dropped the cup in a nearby trash can. "Thank you."

"My pleasure." He drank from his cup, grimaced, and tossed it to join my discarded cup. "If that was Darjeeling, I'll eat my hat." He looked up and down the street. "Did you have a direction in mind? Or do you want to check her usual spots?"

"Let's go this way." I retraced my steps to where Horatio waited.

Horatio bounded away.

I followed the light of his tail as he slowed and took a corner down an alley. The walk reminded me of Luella's fateful pursuit of Zephyr through the backstreets of downtown.

Oliver kept pace without a complaint or a request for an explanation.

The alley led to a warehouse that had seen better days. Pieces of plywood covered the opening where oversized doors once stood. A smaller, intact door stood ajar.

Horatio dashed to the open door.

"I'm going to look inside there," I said.

"Why would she—"

"I think I heard her voice." I hadn't, but it gave me a plausible excuse for going inside. Goosebumps prickled on my arms, and not from the cold. Rich society women didn't usually take meetings in abandoned warehouses. "Do you want to wait here while I look?"

He straightened. His posture somehow made him look even more British. "What if something happened to you in that"—he gestured to the warehouse—"rickety heap of rust and rot?"

Truth be told, I wasn't thrilled about entering the abandoned warehouse by myself. I could be brave, but I wasn't stupid. "Fine," I said. "But keep quiet."

"Of course," he said, already lowering his voice.

We slipped through the door into the darkness of the warehouse. Horatio's fire-tipped tail cast a small circle of magical silver light. Broken glass and bits of old machinery littered the floor. We picked our way through the mess as carefully as we could.

Voices carried from a far corner of the vast room.

I retreated behind a hulking machine and drew Oliver beside me. Our breaths fogged the air.

Mrs. Millefleur's imperious tones snapped into focus. "You haven't given me enough time."

Another voice, too soft to identify or distinguish, murmured a response I couldn't hear. I could, however, hear Mrs. Millefleur's reply: "I can handle this my own way."

Raindrops struck the tin roof, one by one at first, then all at once in a deafening torrent that obliterated any chance of hearing another word.

8

If we stayed where we were, we were likely to get caught eavesdropping. I tugged at Oliver's jacket sleeve and jerked my head toward the direction we'd come from.

Horatio preceded us with feline grace, and I followed as quickly as I could. The noisy rain covered our hasty retreat through the warehouse.

Outside, Oliver stopped to reposition the door to the exact gap at which it had stood when we entered.

We ran through the downpour. Horatio's taillight burned brightly, undimmed by the rain. I'd left my jacket in the truck and had nothing to protect me from getting soaked to the skin.

After we rounded the corner away from the warehouse, Oliver pulled me under a store awning. He whipped off his black suit jacket and placed it on my shoulders.

I touched the fabric and marveled at its elegant drape. The scent of fine, old-fashioned cologne temporarily scrambled my senses. Then I shook myself. What was I thinking? "Here," I said. "I don't need this." I shrugged off the jacket and held it out.

"Nonsense. You're shivering." He cut me a look full of amusement. "Besides, I have a hat, and you don't. Unless you want that, too." He lifted his hat as if he would place it on my head.

"It's fine," I said. I hastily slung the jacket back over my shoulders and pulled it snug like a wrap. "Any idea why your boss is taking meetings in an abandoned warehouse?"

"None whatsoever."

Horatio sat at my feet and looked up at me with a curious expression in his golden eyes.

"What?" I said, challenging Horatio to offer his kitty opinion before realizing that, to Oliver, it looked like I was talking to my feet.

Oliver raised an eyebrow. "I beg your pardon?"

"Nothing," I said. I glared at the rain in lieu of kicking myself for making such an idiotic error.

Oliver held his hand outside the awning. "Feels like it's slowing down. Fancy a run for it?"

I heard his words, but didn't respond. Something didn't add up. Why would he follow me into an abandoned warehouse, as if sneaking around after local real estate magnates was a normal thing to do? Did he have his own reasons to be nosy about Mrs. Millefleur's activities?

Or maybe ... he was humoring me because he was *flirting* with me.

A treacherous voice in my mind whispered: *Why not both?*

There was something I was missing. I was sure of it.

"Rose?"

His voice made me jump.

He had a politely quizzical expression on his face. "Should we not depart? If my employer should see us together, so close to her rendezvous, she might think we were spying on her."

Horatio gave a warning hiss.

Oliver's gaze flicked to the side. "Too late. She's coming up the street."

He was right. Mrs. Millefleur had probably seen us already. I had mere seconds to do something—anything—that would shock the hell out her and drive any thoughts of spying from her head. I seized Oliver's shoulders. "How do you feel about kissing?"

His eyebrows shot up. "Oh, I'm highly in favor of it."

I pulled him forward and pressed my lips to his. The sudden change of balance made both of us stumble, but his hands on my back steadied me. The scent of rain mingled with the taste of tea on his lips. Oliver's kiss made my blood sing.

The sound of Mrs. Millefleur's heels echoed briskly from the surrounding buildings as she approached.

When I was sure she'd seen an eyeful, I released Oliver and tried to pretend I wasn't breathing hard. "Hi, Mrs. Millefleur. Didn't expect to see you on this fine day."

She eyed the churning sky, then looked at Oliver and me. Her eyes widened as she registered Horatio's presence. "Rose. How nice to see you again. I see you've met my chauffeur." Her gaze swept over him and stopped where my red lipstick stained his lips.

Oliver cleared his throat. "Rose and I decided to go for coffee, ma'am."

"Coffee?" Her expression went from disapproving to frosty. "In future, try to limit your 'coffee' to your own time." Mrs. Millefleur fished a packet of tissues from her small handbag and pulled out a single tissue. She brandished it at Oliver. "You may return to your post. Please take the car to be detailed."

"Of course, ma'am." He accepted the tissue, carefully wiped his lips, and looked quite serious—except for an almost imperceptible wink he aimed in my direction before he walked away.

Mrs. Millefleur and I watched him go.

"I'll thank you not to harass my staff, Rose."

I opened my mouth to object to her framing of the situation, but she wasn't finished.

"It shows a certain ... lack of restraint."

That was rich, coming from someone who threw people off lighthouses.

When she finally looked at me, her cheeks were slightly pink. Had we made the great and powerful Mrs. Millefleur blush?

"I assume you came looking for me. Shall we repair to my office?"

"After you," I said. It was only then I realized I still had Oliver's jacket. I tugged it tighter.

Horatio walked between us. By the time we reached the yellow brick building, the Town Car was gone.

Gladys looked up as we entered Millefleur Properties. "You found her!"

"Yes, she did. Please hold my calls, Gladys."

"You got it, boss lady."

I followed Mrs. Millefleur down the hall to her office.

She took a seat in a throne-like leather chair behind a wide desk crafted of some dark and expensive-looking wood. Built-in bookshelves of the same wood lined the wall behind her.

I sat in a smaller leather chair. Horatio settled in my lap.

Mrs. Millefleur's gaze went to Horatio. "So, you found yourself a familiar."

Her peremptory tone needled me into saying the first thing that popped into my mind. "Yes, I did. Where's yours, by the way?"

She waved a hand dismissively. "Those manifestations are a sign of weakness. Of a lack of discipline."

"In other words, you have one but you're afraid to show it off?"

Real anger flashed across her face. "You have no idea what you're talking about."

I didn't know what the sore spot was, but I'd certainly struck it. "That's why I'm here. I want to learn."

She sat back. Her fingers curled over the arms of the chair, and for the first time, I noticed her nails were bitten almost to the quick. It seemed incongruous with her otherwise perfect presentation. "*Now* you want to learn?" A faint smirk lifted the corner of her lips. "What happened?"

"Life." I patted Horatio calmly, more calmly than I really felt. "Life happened."

"How droll." She stood and paced. "Let me guess. Someone in your life is in trouble. You want to help them. You want to ... 'abracadabra' your way out of it. But your magic is limited and clumsy." She speared me with a look. "Not to mention ineffective to the purpose."

Heat crawled up my cheeks, but I matched her stare. "Something like that."

"And for that, I should reveal all my secrets? After you refused my offer of teaching in the first place?" Her light, musical laugh was somehow worse than a villainous one.

"I'm glad I amuse you."

"Oh, without a doubt."

"So you won't do it, then?"

"Who said I wouldn't?"

"You did."

"Not at all. You misunderstand me."

"Enlighten me, then."

She returned to her seat. "I offered to teach you. The offer stands. I ask only that you remember this favor in future; that I may call upon you at need." She steepled her fingers and looked at me across the desk.

My mind replayed the night at the lighthouse, and the strange conversation I'd half-overheard in the abandoned warehouse. This was the woman who'd pushed Raphael off the lighthouse with one hand, and with the other, deeded an entire house to Luella. She had her own agenda and couldn't be trusted—but she had the knowledge I needed. "Within reason," I said.

Her perfect white teeth flashed. "Then—we have a deal."

9

I could hardly wait to tell my friends what had happened. At work the following day, we synchronized our lunch breaks and headed out on foot to nearby Fortunella Park, where we would not be overheard.

By the time we entered the park under a high canopy of tall oaks, I had brought them up to speed on the events of the previous day. The branches above us created an almost solid green roof, casting the ground below into deep shade. Dangling clumps of Spanish moss swayed in the breeze. We passed a formal white rotunda in favor of our favorite picnic lunch spot: a spacious wooden bench under an arbor covered in star jasmine.

Zephyr and Horatio dashed away across the grass and chased each other around the coquina boulders.

Pepper rummaged in her lunch bag and retrieved a sandwich. She unwrapped it, but instead of biting into it, she waved it through the air to emphasize her words. "Look at those two clowns. They're so funny. I wonder what my familiar will be?" She took a bite of her sandwich.

Luella unscrewed a thermos and tipped it back.

Pepper finished her bite and continued. "Queenie's like me, you know—she doesn't have one yet, either." Her gaze tracked Zephyr and Horatio as they played. "What do you think Mrs. Millefleur's familiar is?"

My eyebrows lifted in surprise. It hadn't even occurred to me to wonder what Mrs. Millefleur's familiar might be. I absentmindedly fished in my partitioned container for a cube of cheese while I puzzled out the question. "Another cat, maybe?"

"I bet it's a bird of prey," said Luella. "Something regal and intimidating, like a hawk—or an owl."

"That'd be a hoot! Get it?" Pepper elbowed me.

I nearly choked on my cheese. "I get it."

Pepper settled back, a thoughtful expression on her face. "Do you really trust her, after everything she pulled?"

"No. But what choice do I have?"

"At least she has a hot chauffeur you can hang around with."

"I'm not looking to hang around with him."

"Of course you're not." Pepper made eye contact with Luella and wiggled her eyebrows like Groucho Marx.

"Just because you two are love fools doesn't mean I have to be one, too."

"Who said anything about love? Just grab him and kiss him every once in a while. Good for your health." Pepper winked so broadly it looked like she was having an eye problem.

Luella chuckled.

I attempted to wrest back control of the conversation. "The real concern here—"

"Other than hot chauffeurs—"

"Shut up," I said cordially. "The *real* concern"—I eyed Pepper, who widened her eyes innocently—"is what I'm going to do to help Izzy get that house."

"She's got a good lawyer, right?" asked Luella.

I nodded. "My soon-to-be ex-brother-in-law is such a devious little bastard, though. I don't trust that he won't come up with something."

Pepper tapped her chin. "She shouldn't stay away from the house too long. He might try to use her absence to prove she doesn't want to live there."

"That's what my sister said. Can he really do that?"

"Depends on the judge you get."

I rubbed my forehead. "We need him out. We need to . . . I don't know. Make him not *want* the house, or something."

We stared out into the park as we finished our lunches, each of us lost in thought.

Horatio climbed to the top of the highest boulder. He sat and surveyed the park as if he were the king of the mountain. Zephyr ran in circles around the base of the giant rock.

"Hang on." Luella stood abruptly and paced in front of the arbor. "Hold the phones. This is going to sound crazy—"

Pepper leaned forward. "I love crazy!"

"Rose, your sister needed a break because he was driving her crazy on purpose, am I right?"

I nodded. Where was this going?

Luella whirled to face us, her hands spread wide in a gesture of excitement. "You have to turn the tables. *Move in with him.*"

I blinked. "What?"

"Move in with him! Don't abandon the field! Get your sister and her kids, get your stuff, and march right back over there. Drive *him* crazy. See if he can pull anything when you're around to cramp his style."

"I bet he won't!" said Pepper. "He sounds like a coward to me."

My mouth hung open. "But—" I paused. My gaze strayed to Horatio, the king of the mountain, grooming himself on his high perch. "But he'll just ride it out."

Pepper waved her hands through the air. "You're not thinking big enough. You're a *witch*. Surely you can do something to make him want to leave."

"And we can come over and visit, too," added Luella.

"*Three* witches in the house!" said Pepper.

I looked at Luella. A tiny spark of hope ignited.

Luella's eyes sparkled with mischief, and in that moment, she looked more like her mother than ever. "Why not?"

Pepper leaped to her feet. "Ride-or-Die Witches, assemble!"

I couldn't suppress a laugh. "Pepper, not so loud!"

"What?" She cast a theatrical look around. "There's no one here."

Zephyr loped into the arbor, bringing with her a fresh, cold breeze, and sat at Luella's side. Horatio followed in his own way, by disappearing from his rocky throne in a flash and reappearing on my shoulders. "Well, hello there, your majesty." I gave his head a little scratch, then stood up with my friends.

"Hands in the middle," said Luella. She stuck out her hand, palm down.

"Count of three." Pepper placed her hand on Luella's.

A smile fought its way onto my lips. I laid my hand over theirs. "All right. One, two, three—"

"Ride-or-die!" we cried.

Zephyr barked enthusiastically. Horatio pretended to be unaffected; instead, he batted a lock of my hair, then bit it.

"Horatio!" Pepper put her hands on her hips in mock outrage. "Show some respect."

"It's not in his nature." Luella gave me a pointed look. "Like someone else I know."

"What do you mean?" I said. "I'm highly respectful."

Pepper and Luella snorted.

"Of those who deserve it." I gave Horatio an extra scratch because I respected his lack of respect.

We gathered our things and returned to Suntan Queen before our break time was up. After we passed through the revolving door, Pepper and Luella veered away to the office side of the building, and Horatio and Zephyr scampered away on their own. I continued to the factory floor.

Queenie stood off to the side of the machinery, a white lab coat over her richly colored sweater and patterned slacks. She pivoted on her high heels. "Rose, darling! You're back from lunch?"

"Back and ready to roll."

She approached me and laid a hand on my bicep. Her fingers closed like iron pincers, and her gaze searched mine.

She leaned in. "I could practically hear you coming—your blood was rushing around like wild."

I still wasn't used to the way Queenie could read emotional states like a normal person would read a thermometer. "Was it?"

Queenie released my arm and gave me a look. "Don't kid a kidder, darling. Now tell Aunt Queenie all about it." My boss draped her arm over my shoulder and steered me away from the machinery.

I liked Queenie a lot—I really did—but the combination of her being both my employer *and* a powerful witch was enough to set my defenses on high. And of course she would be able to sense that on some level, which made the whole interaction even more uncomfortable. "It's nothing, Queenie. Just some personal stuff I'm dealing with."

"Personal stuff is my specialty."

"I have to get back to the factory floor …"

"Nonsense. I own the factory floor, and I say you don't need to be on it until you've unburdened yourself."

I sighed. Clearly I wasn't getting away unscathed. "My sister is having some divorce difficulties, and I'm also a bit nervous about training with your loose cannon of an associate."

"Hilda?"

I nodded.

Queenie's heels clicked as we walked. "Do you know how I knew you were feeling agitated?"

"You could sense it"—I looked around, making sure no one was in earshot—"with your magic."

"Exactly, darling. Now, I don't know the details of your situation, but you would do well to cultivate the same ability. *Tout suite*. Get Hilda to show you that before you do anything else."

"Why?" Given the choice, I would have preferred to practice blowing things up rather than focus on the nuance of reading people.

Queenie gave me a little shake. "Because you can't solve everything by setting it on fire."

"It would be simpler that way."

She laughed. "Get back to work, Rose. Try not to burn down the factory."

I sketched a bow like a player on a stage. "Yes, ma'am."

10

After I hung up my lab coat for the day, I checked my dog-training profile for new messages. If I had any potential new clients, I might be able to spin that into some extra money. My job at Suntan Queen paid well enough, but I hadn't scraped together the down payment on the cabin by resting on my laurels—side hustles had been second nature all my life.

I locked down a date and time with a client and tucked the phone away. I needed both hands free to make the truck cabin ready for a canine passenger.

In the Suntan Queen parking lot, I unlocked the truck and swung the doors wide. Horatio jumped in and draped himself over the dashboard to watch me work.

I opened the cargo box in the truck bed and retrieved a mat for the seat and a sturdy dog harness. I picked up a Millefleur Properties pen, a candy wrapper, and a brush that had somehow wedged itself between the seats. I laid the mat on the seat. I clipped the harness in place and tugged on it to make sure it was secure.

Then I saw Oliver's jacket, which had fallen to the floor behind the front seat. I picked it up, shook it out, and was about to toss it in the cargo box when I felt a flexible, card-like object through the fabric. Intrigued, I rifled the pockets. The outside pockets were empty, but the inside pocket contained a thick white business card. The front of the card was embossed in black ink with the name Oliver Hawthorne, followed by a phone number.

I knew I should drop off the jacket at Millefleur Properties. Better yet, I should have hurled it out the truck window as I drove past rather than entangle myself with the chauffeur again, because whatever had come over me that day was a mistake not to be repeated. I did not need any further complications in my life.

On second thought …

How would I avoid Oliver, anyway? He'd be ferrying Mrs. Millefleur to and from our appointments no matter where they took place.

I lifted the jacket and held the fine, cool fabric under my nose. The fragrance of sandalwood, or perhaps cedar, brought an unexpected surge of heat to my skin.

Good thing Queenie wasn't around to notice.

I smoothed out the jacket and folded it on the seat. Horatio jumped down from the dash and curled up on the jacket. "Don't get too cozy," I said. "I'm not keeping it."

He meowed with a questioning tone.

"No, I'm not going to call him." I retrieved the card from my pocket and ran my fingertip over the embossed letters and numbers. "That would be silly." I tossed the card down.

The wind caught it and sent it tumbling away. I scrambled to catch it. With the card in hand, I wavered. Why should I hesitate if the kiss meant nothing? I knew what I was doing. I was completely in control.

I would just send a quick text.

I edged onto the seat next to Horatio and punched the digits into the phone, followed by a message: *Hello, Oliver. It's Rose. I just realized I still have your jacket.*

Simple, businesslike, and efficient. I hit the send button.

Hello, Rose, he replied.

Goosebumps prickled my arms. "Damn this cold weather." I slid all the way into the truck, slammed the door, and turned on the heat. I plugged in the phone for some background music. Robert Smith's voice filled the air with the chorus of "Friday I'm in Love."

I quickly yanked the cord out. "Shut up, Robert."

Oliver sent another message: *I would be happy to retrieve it at your convenience.*

The heat was blowing directly on my cheeks, toasting them to a healthy blush, judging by their appearance in the rearview mirror. I slapped the airflow controls to knock the hot draft away from my face.

Horatio crept across the seat and peered at the phone.

"What do I say?" I smoothed the warm fur on his back. "I should just drop it off—right, Horatio?"

The cat gently bit the side of my hand.

"Ow. Well, when you put it that way—" I quickly typed a new message: *Did you want to meet up? If so, where?*

Horatio settled alongside me and purred like a very small freight train.

Oliver's message arrived with a buzz. *May I get you another coffee? Our last hot beverage was unfortunately brief.*

Now that was an understatement. *Coffee it is. Or tea, as the case may be,* I wrote. *Same place?*

Nearly, he replied. *How about the Christmas market downtown? There may even be cider.*

Talk about living dangerously, I typed. *I accept your offer.* We agreed to meet Saturday morning, on Oliver's day off.

I headed back to the cabin. Inside, I found Izzy supervising Astrid and Sadie as they toasted marshmallows in the fireplace. Horatio picked his way over to the fireplace and curled up against the andiron.

Izzy studied the sooty burn marks on the stones. "What happened here? Did you try to burn a Christmas tree in the fireplace?"

"Just because Christmas isn't my favorite holiday doesn't mean I set trees on fire out of spite." I looked around. "Where's Braveheart?"

Izzy gestured toward the backyard. "I let him out when we got home."

I grabbed a stick and speared a marshmallow on the tip, then let the marshmallow hover above the coals until it blackened.

"Aunt Rose!" said Sadie. "You burned it."

"I like it well-done." I blew on the marshmallow before biting through the crust into the molten interior.

Astrid took careful bites of her perfectly golden-brown marshmallow. When she finished, she twirled the empty stick like a baton. Strands of her hair snagged on the sticky residue. "Oops. Hair-mallows." She tugged the stick until it released.

"Good as new," I said. "Want to try a burned one?"

Astrid and Sadie looked at each other, then shook their heads.

When Izzy finally confiscated the bag of marshmallows and sent the girls off, we had the living room to ourselves. "Speaking of spite," I said, "Pepper says to make sure you don't leave the house for too long. She said it might look bad to the judge."

Izzy grimaced. "I know. She's right. We're going back tomorrow."

I plunged another marshmallow into the fire and imagined it was Damon's face.

It ignited.

I knew better than to wave it around—I pulled it out of the fire and blew sharply to put it out.

Izzy continued. "I think Damon's been getting some weird divorce advice off the internet."

"Typical. He probably thinks he's the cleverest man alive."

Izzy squeezed the marshmallow bag too tightly. "Did I make a mistake? Should I not have taken a little break?"

"I don't think you made a mistake. I think you did what you had to do to stay sane. You've been away from the house for a couple of days, not a couple of months." I toyed with the marshmallow toasting stick, weighing my words before I spoke. "Luella had an idea."

"Good, because I'm fresh out."

"She suggested I move in with you."

Izzy's eyes widened. "Move in?"

"Until the settlement—or until Damon leaves of his own volition."

She studied my face. "Why are you smiling? What's going on in that head of yours?"

"I was thinking about how Damon probably wouldn't love living with your dear sister Rose."

Izzy burst out laughing. "No, he would not. I don't think he's prepared for the full Rose experience."

"Who is?" I tugged the bag of marshmallows out of Izzy's hands and pulled a plump marshmallow from the bag. An impulse to tell Izzy about my magical powers struck me. It would have been so simple to demonstrate—all I had to do was light up a marshmallow. Was it too much for her to handle, though? She didn't need to worry about anything else. My gaze shifted from the marshmallow, to the fire, and finally to Horatio.

Horatio's golden eyes reflected the dancing flames, but gave me no answers.

I speared the marshmallow on the stick—and chickened out. "What do you think? Shall we turn the tables?"

Izzy's brow furrowed as she stared into the fire. A look of resolve settled over her features. "Let's do it." She held up her hand for a high five. "Sister power!"

I high-fived her. "Sister power. We got this." We settled back on the couch, shoulder to shoulder, basking in the warmth of the fire together.

11

Mrs. Millefleur arrived the next morning in her white Town Car.

I peeked through the curtains as Oliver opened her door. Mrs. Millefleur stepped out of the car and buttoned her suit jacket.

Oliver's gaze roamed over the front of the cabin. He shut the door for Mrs. Millefleur before returning to the driver's side.

She squared her shoulders and marched up to the porch.

After she knocked, I waited. No point in having her think I was too eager. I counted out the seconds, then pulled the door open.

She marched inside without a greeting. "You're sure no one is here?"

"Positive. Well, other than your chauffeur."

"Oliver will stay with the car."

Awkward silence fell. I gestured to the couch. "Please, have a seat."

We sat on opposite ends. Braveheart trotted out of the hallway and surveyed the living room scene with doggy curiosity. Mrs. Millefleur quickly drew her legs up.

I rose and went to Braveheart. "Don't worry. He's a good boy. You can put your legs down."

She kept her gaze locked on Braveheart. "You're sure?"

I nodded.

Horatio appeared in the fireplace in a flash of silver light. He picked his way over the cold ashes, stopping to shake his little black paws as he went. He approached Braveheart and tapped the dog's massive shoulder.

Braveheart obediently flopped on the floor.

Horatio curled up—the small spoon to Braveheart's big spoon—and let out a contented purr.

Mrs. Millefleur slowly lowered her feet to the floor. "Your cat seems to think he's all right."

"They're buddies." I returned to the couch, and another awkward silence descended.

Mrs. Millefleur fiddled with her necklace, then spoke. "Perhaps you should tell me more about your sister's situation, so that I might determine what skills might serve you best." Her formal tone made it sound like we were having tea at Buckingham Palace.

Had I mentioned that the situation had to do with my sister? I must have. Otherwise, how would she have known? I shook my head to clear it, then related Izzy's situation and my involvement in it.

Mrs. Millefleur leaned forward, steepled her fingers, and listened.

When I finished speaking, she stood and paced in front of the fireplace. "It was unwise to play tricks on your sister's husband."

I opened my mouth to protest, but she continued before I could get the words out—which was probably a good thing, because some of them weren't polite.

"Don't get your back up. I didn't say it was wrong; I said it was unwise. It could have been done better." She pierced me with a look. "Did you accomplish anything from it?"

"I—"

"Of course you didn't. You weren't thinking ahead; you were only thinking of what would satisfy you in that moment."

I felt a mulish look settle over my face. It didn't help that she was absolutely right.

"You want him out, do you not?"

I nodded.

"Then we will not resort to silly magic tricks that serve no purpose. Agreed?"

"Agreed." I sounded like Astrid when she was in one of her grumpy moods.

"Rather than setting your brother-in-law on fire, I suggest we begin with something a little more subtle." She ceased pacing and sat.

As I looked into her dark eyes, I realized all over again that I was dealing with the same witch that had hypnotized and kidnapped Raphael. With that kind of résumé, what *wouldn't* she do?

Come to think of it, what wouldn't *I* do for the sake of helping my sister?

I ignored the moral misgivings; after all, I was doing this for the right reasons.

Mrs. Millefleur removed a necklace with a large orange stone and set it in her lap.

"What's that?" I asked.

"My fire opal. It is an artifact that channels fire magic, among other things."

"Can I see it?"

She held it out.

I picked it up with great care. The orange gem spun on its chain. The enchantment of the gem was so palpable that I wanted to cradle it in my hands and press it against my skin just to feel its power. "Where can I get one of these?"

Mrs. Millefleur took hold of the pendant. I held onto the chain a beat longer than I should have, then released it. She held the pendant in the palm of her hand and studied it, as if memorizing the face of an old friend before a long journey. Her gaze moved from the stone to me.

I shifted uncomfortably. I didn't like the sensation of being examined. Or—worse—being judged and found wanting.

Mrs. Millefleur weighed the necklace in her hand, then held it out again. The gem winked and glittered. "Take it."

I reached for it eagerly, then hesitated. "Why would you give me this?"

"You need it more than I do."

I didn't know whether to feel insulted that she thought my powers needed boosting, or gratitude that she trusted me with such a treasure. A messy mix of the two feelings twinged my gut. And as much as I wanted it, I didn't want her to feel like she had to give it up. "Are you sure?"

She opened the necklace chain. "Turn around."

I changed my position.

She passed the necklace around my neck and closed the clasp in the back. She freed my hair from underneath the chain—an oddly motherly gesture—and the necklace fell into place. "There," she said.

I turned to face her again. I gripped the pendant in my hand; the warp and weft of its power fizzed through me, along with an impression that drifted from Mrs. Millefleur like smoke from a blown-out candle, faint but perceptible: *So much like me.*

Was it my thought or hers?

She stared into the fireplace, her face unreadable. "Why don't you make a fire before we begin? There's a chill in the air."

I kneeled in front of the fireplace and extended my hand. Silver fire shot from my fingertips and boiled into the fireplace, igniting the leftover logs from the previous day. My new necklace glowed in the firelight.

"Much better. I miss being able to do that." She rubbed her hands together. "Let's begin. Come closer."

I took a seat on the couch. We angled ourselves to face each other.

"First we will practice mind reading."

I shied back before I could stop myself. The notion of letting Mrs. Millefleur into my thoughts made my hair stand on end.

"Calm down," she said. "I want you to read *my* mind."

"Oh."

Mrs. Millefleur rolled her eyes. "I promise I will do nothing to discomfort, or harm, or even *annoy* you. Will that be acceptable?"

I reminded myself that I was doing all of this for a reason—a very good and noble reason that was certainly worth a small amount of risk—and nodded my agreement.

She acknowledged it with a brisk nod of her own. "That's settled, then. Look in my eyes. It may feel a bit strange, but remember that I am not making you do anything; I am only guiding you." Silver fire flashed in her eyes.

I remained aware of my surroundings, but in some undefinable way I went *under*. Mrs. Millefleur's voice came to me as if from a great distance. Then I realized her lips weren't moving—she wasn't speaking to me, she was *thinking* at me.

Rose, can you hear me?

My thoughts swirled like fog before I found the coherence to reply. *I hear you.*

Look into my eyes. Reach for the fire within my mind.

I concentrated, but felt nothing.

Push harder.

I don't want to hurt you, I thought.

You won't. Stop resisting your power.

I gritted my teeth and pushed my awareness to its limits. Something snapped into focus like a field of stars or a map lit with points of silver fire: Mrs. Millefleur's mind.

Her next command came through with bell-like clarity: *Feel the shape of my thoughts.*

Impressions rolled through me. First, a view from the top of the Sparkle Beach lighthouse. A bottle of champagne, its green glass catching the last rays of the setting sun. Then Luella's face, lit with anger and determination. Luella again, falling and falling—then flying.

And underneath it all... fear.

What could you possibly have to be afraid of? I pressed against the points of light and ran up against a wall. *What aren't you letting me see?*

With that thought, the dreamlike vision vanished. I blinked. "Mrs. Millefleur?"

She didn't meet my gaze. She was looking at Braveheart and Horatio, who remained in their snuggly pile near the fire, with a tinge of sadness. "You don't have to see everything to know that my motives were not what you thought."

"You can trust me," I said.

"Oh, Rose. Of course I can. Despite your pretenses to darkness, you're nothing but a walking mass of tender feelings."

A wordless squawk of protest popped out of my mouth.

"Regardless, my trust in you is not the issue. If I withhold information, it is for your protection."

There was clearly no point in pursuing the subject. I rubbed my arms, like a dry bath to remove the traces of someone else's memories. "That was weird, seeing someone else's thoughts."

"You will not find it so, with practice. I suggest you start with your brother-in-law." A humorless smile tightened her lips. "Wars are not won by the weak of stomach."

12

I almost smiled back before I realized that Mrs. Millefleur could have been doing a bit of light mind reading on any of us all along. Would I have even noticed if she had?

She'd said *your sister's situation* as if I had mentioned it when we spoke in her office.

But I hadn't. I never said it was my sister. It could have been my dentist, or me, or the Wizard of Oz, for all she knew.

I didn't need Mrs. Millefleur's help to find that starry mind-map again. I reached for her thoughts with my magic, determined to confirm my suspicions …

And ran into an electrified brick wall.

"Ow!" I rubbed my eyes. "What'd you do that for?"

Amusement danced in her eyes. "You didn't think I'd notice your clumsy attempt to poke around in my head?"

"You've read my mind before, haven't you?"

"Don't be simple. I keep tabs on everyone. That's what I do."

"Well, stop it."

"When you become competent, you will be able to stop it yourself." She raised an eyebrow. "Also, you need to work on your technique. Even a non-magical dolt like your brother-in-law will be able to sense you blundering around like that. Easy does it, that's the way." As if she was advising me on how to make a perfect pie crust.

I ignored a pang from my bruised ego and whatever moral fiber I had left. "Fine. What's next?"

"You seem more or less competent at starting fires. Have you tried putting them out?"

"A little."

"Have you tested your range?"

"No."

"What *have* you been doing?"

"Other than setting Damon's pants on fire? Not much. Oh, wait—I tried to warm up my clothes on a cold morning."

"You *tried*?"

"Hey, it mostly worked. I only burned a small spot on my jacket."

She gave me a skeptical look.

"Don't judge me," I said. "It's been busy around here. Look"—I stretched my hand toward the fire—"I'm practicing right now." I exerted my power and willed the fire to go out.

Sparks exploded in a hundred flying points of orange light, and the fire burned higher than ever. Braveheart dashed away down the hall. Horatio, left without his big spoon, sat up in a huff and began washing his paws with great indignance.

"I wouldn't have started with a fire that large," Mrs. Millefleur said.

"Now you tell me." I stamped out the handful of sparks that had escaped the fireplace.

"Why don't we take a walk? 'Fresh air, clear mind,' as my husband used to say."

I'd never heard her mention a husband before, although it was obvious she must have had one, thanks to her insistence on the title of *Mrs*—but her use of the past tense indicated her husband had passed away. "Sounds like a wise fellow."

"That he was."

When she didn't elaborate, I filled the silence. "The ground is pretty soft and sandy around here. I'm not sure your shoes will work."

She glanced at her two-inch heels. "I shall retrieve an alternate pair from the car."

"You carry extra pairs of shoes?"

"Doesn't anyone with sense?"

I let that remark slide. We left the cabin, and Oliver leaped out of the car on sight of Mrs. Millefleur.

"Oliver, kindly retrieve my sneakers."

"Yes, ma'am."

What was a dapper middle-aged man like him doing as a chauffeur? Shouldn't he be married with six children and a corner office? On the other hand, I had neither children nor a corner office—the lab didn't count—so it seemed hypocritical to judge. Instead, I admired the way he presented my mentor with a pair of sparkling white trainers and socks. He was deferential without being meek.

"Thank you, Oliver," she said.

"You're quite welcome, ma'am." He looked at me and touched his hat—and with all the certainty of a newspaper edge beginning to burn, I knew he was thinking of our kiss. "Miss Rose."

"Oliver." Despite the cold, I felt a warmth that had nothing to do with the pale winter sun.

Mrs. Millefleur cleared her throat. "That will be all." She held her sneakers in one hand and put the other on my bicep to steer me toward the cabin.

"You don't have to herd me like a sheep, you know," I said when we were far enough that Oliver couldn't hear. "I'm a grown woman."

"Could have fooled me," she replied. Inside, she removed her heels and replaced them with the socks and sneakers.

"Are you still mad I kissed your chauffeur?"

She sat up straight. "I was never *mad*. I found it inappropriate."

The contrast between her stuffy bearing and her utterly goofy white sneakers nearly made me laugh, when suddenly, without conscious effort, my magic slipped beneath her facade and found the feeling underneath it: *protectiveness*.

She felt protective of Oliver.

I had no time to process this new thought, because she jumped to her feet and quick-marched down the hall like a mall walker on a second cup of coffee. I hurried after her. "Wait up!"

She breezed out the back door, calling "Fresh air, clear mind! Do try to keep up."

I shut the back door securely to make sure Braveheart didn't wander off—Horatio would follow or not, if he felt like it.

Mrs. Millefleur held open the back gate, the last remaining barrier to Black Bear Ridge.

I hustled through and shut it behind us. "What's the plan?"

"We walk."

We tramped through the forest, our steps ruffling the brown pine needles on the ground. The pine branches above swayed in the wind, and the air smelled of pine sap and sand.

"How far?" I asked after we'd walked for a few minutes.

She rolled her eyes. "Were you like this in school?"

"Like what?"

"Questioning. Resistant."

"No. I was much worse."

"I don't know how Queenie puts up with you," she said.

"I'm good at my job."

"If I were her, I'd fire you anyway. Just to save aggravation."

"I wouldn't put it past you," I said. "Considering what you've done in the past."

She was unperturbed. "I did what was necessary. So will you, when the time comes." She stopped in a small clearing ringed by palmettos. "This should be fine. Enough distance from other people." She rubbed her hands together. "Let's see what you can do."

I surveyed the clearing. "I don't think I want to start a forest fire …"

"Nonsense. We'll just practice heat sensing. Stand here." She indicated the middle of the clearing.

I stepped to where she pointed.

"Close your eyes."

I obeyed. After reading her thoughts in the cabin, I couldn't very well get squeamish about closing my eyes in a clearing.

"Turn your senses outward and look for sources of heat."

Facing out into the deep forest, I perceived nothing at first. Then I saw a burst of bright orange, like an afterimage. It appeared in the direction of Mrs. Millefleur's voice. "Is that you?"

"Does it move when I do?"

The pine needles crunched under her sneakers. The reddish afterimage dragged across my awareness in the same direction as the sound. Delight rushed through me. "Yes, it does!" A second afterimage blazed in my peripheral vision—smaller, faster, and somehow more intense than Mrs. Millefleur's heat signature. "Wait—what's that?"

As soon as I spoke, the second, smaller heat signature shot away through the trees and vanished. I opened my eyes. "There's something up there."

She peered into the trees. "Probably a squirrel. Try again."

I squeezed my eyes shut and concentrated. The small, orange ball of light crept into my field of perception again. I stealthily cracked one eye open, but whatever it was, it took off before I could identify it. "Damn."

Mrs. Millefleur patted my shoulder awkwardly, as if she'd never performed that particular motion before. "Not to worry. You'll improve with practice. Eventually, you won't have to close your eyes. You'll be able to sense heat and see at the same time."

"Can you still sense heat?" I didn't add *since you lost your powers*, because it wasn't my intention to wound her.

"I cannot."

I nodded. Then I patted her shoulder almost as awkwardly as she'd patted mine.

She looked at me like I'd grown an extra head.

I withdrew my hand.

13

On Saturday morning, I poured a cup of black coffee and sat at the kitchen table to down half of it in one too-hot gulp. Horatio curled up in my lap and provided a welcome source of warmth as the caffeine fired my groggy synapses to life. *Oliver. Jacket. Christmas market.*

I slammed the half-empty mug onto the table. I could have given Oliver his jacket the day before, when Mrs. Millefleur came to visit, and cancelled the date. I banged my head on the table. *Stupid, stupid, stupid.*

Wait—why was I even calling it a date? It wasn't a date. That hadn't been a real kiss, just a kiss of convenience.

I banged my head on the table a few more times for good measure.

Horatio yowled with annoyance and jumped down from my lap.

"Aunt Rose?"

I sat up like I'd been zapped.

Sadie peered at me from around the corner. "Aunt Rose, you okay?"

I smoothed my hair. "I'm fine. Did I wake you?"

She shook her head and shuffled into the kitchen in her fuzzy slippers. She ran her small hands over my black leather bag, which sat on the table rather than in its customary place on a hook by the door. "You going somewhere?"

"Aunt Rose is going to return someone's jacket."

She absorbed this information, then cocked her head. "Couldn't you just mail it to her?"

"Him. And no, this way's faster." Doubt creeped into my voice as I spoke.

Sadie raised her eyebrows. "Is that what you're wearing?"

I looked down at myself. "Why?"

She plucked at my sleeve. "Not very festive."

"I don't do festive."

She patted my shoulder. "Don't worry, Aunt Rose. We'll help you."

"No, that's not necessary—"

But Sadie had already run out of the room. She returned moments later with Astrid in tow.

Astrid eyed me up and down. "Sadie's right. You need help."

They seized my wrists and hauled me out of my seat. I looked around, hoping that Izzy would come to my rescue and call them off. "Where's your mother?"

"Showering," said Sadie as they dragged me down the hall. Inside my bedroom, they threw open the closet doors and plunged their hands into the sea of black.

Astrid retrieved two black blouses and held them at arm's length. "I respect your commitment to the whole 'goth' aesthetic, Aunt Rose, but don't you own *anything* that's not black?"

Sadie pulled open a drawer and rifled through my folded clothes. "Black, black, black, black, black."

I lunged for the dresser. "Don't go through grown-ups' dresser drawers, Sadie."

"Why?" said Sadie.

"Because that's where I keep my bear traps."

Astrid smirked.

Sadie shrugged and joined her sister by the closet. "What about this?" She plucked a crimson scarf from where I'd shoved it. "This is pretty."

Astrid took it and draped it over my shoulders. "Matches your lipstick."

"It's not that cold. I don't need a scarf—"

"Quiet." Astrid folded her arms and regarded me. "Needs something else."

"Mommy has a fancy hair comb. I'll get it." Sadie skipped away. She brought back a decorative comb encrusted with dark red crystals.

Astrid took the comb and slid it into my hair. She gave a sharp nod. "Better."

Sadie adjusted the red scarf. "Much better."

I examined my appearance in the mirror. "Luella's mama would be thrilled someone made me 'put some color on.'"

My sister's voice carried from down the hall. "Where is everyone?" Izzy arrived in the doorway, her hair still damp from a shower. "What are you all doing in Aunt Rose's room?"

Sadie beamed. "We're teaching Aunt Rose to get dressed, Mommy!"

"She has a date," said Astrid.

"No, I don't." I fiddled with the position of the scarf to get the drape just right.

Izzy stifled a laugh. "Rose?"

"I'm returning some dude's jacket, all right? Leave me be."

The girls collapsed into giggles.

Izzy straightened her expression with what appeared to be great effort. "All right. Let Aunt Rose get out of here before she's late for her ... jacket-returning."

"A pack of cards, the lot of you." I marched out of my room, dodged Braveheart, grabbed my bag, and stuffed my feet into my boots. Out in the truck, I waited for Horatio to make an appearance—I'd gotten used to his riding shotgun.

When nothing happened, I rolled my eyes. "Typical cat. Come on, fire kitty."

He appeared on the passenger seat with a pop and a silver flash, twitching his fire-tipped tail before settling in a comfortable curl.

"Good boy." I scratched his head.

The look on his face said it all: *Good boy? Do I look like a dog to you?*

We drove downtown to a large fenced lot located behind one of the old buildings. Green garland studded with red bows draped the fence. I swung the truck into a parking space. I thought Horatio might climb to my shoulders like a second scarf over the red one, but he dashed out of sight as soon as I opened the door. I picked up Oliver's jacket and folded it over my arm.

My boots crunched over the gravel and crushed shells as I made my way over to the Christmas market. Pop-up tents formed neat rows that stretched across the grounds. Every breath of cold air I took to steady my nerves brought with it the scent of sugar-roasted nuts.

Then, I saw him.

Oliver leaned against a tall and skinny palm tree near the fair entrance. Off duty, he wore a well-cut tweed jacket layered over a crimson sweater.

I exhaled in relief. There was nothing to be afraid of—he wasn't my type at all. Too clean cut. If I bothered to be attracted to anyone, it would be someone who wore black, not tweed and sweaters.

Although, on closer inspection, his sweater looked re-markably plush. Like you could sink your fingers into its texture and stay warm for days.

Oliver's eyes lit up as I approached. "Hello there."

"I brought your jacket." The words came out blunter than I intended.

"So you did." He took it carefully and draped it over his arm. "I am eternally grateful."

I froze. I should have said something, anything, even *you're welcome*, but nothing came out of my mouth. My heart beat faster, and I was absurdly sure it would flutter the red scarf with its rapid beats.

Oliver gestured toward the market. "May I get you something to eat? There's the scent of something tempting in the air."

Part of me wanted to make excuses and leave. Part of me gravitated toward Oliver like iron to a magnet. The part of me that said *go for it* wrestled the side of me that said *run away* into submission.

I nodded my acceptance and fell into step with Oliver. We passed a booth of colorful glass ornaments, followed by a table covered with cellophane-wrapped bundles of candy.

I stopped at a larger booth packed with stringed instruments: dulcimers, mandolins, ukuleles, and harps sized to fit on your lap. I stroked a small harp displayed on a stand.

The shopkeeper approached. She smoothed a skirt that wouldn't have been out of place at a Renaissance fair. "Do you play?"

I dropped my hand. "I'm just browsing."

Oliver touched the harp and glanced at the shopkeeper. "May I?"

She gestured permission.

"It's a Gothic harp," he observed. "See the high arch? Different from the Celtic style." He braced the harp against his chest with his left hand and plucked a few strings, producing a warm and sweet tone.

"Do you play?" I asked.

He smiled. "Not in the slightest." He reversed his hold on the harp. "Here, you try."

I gave the harp a dubious look. "My nieces say I'm Goth, but I don't think that's what they meant."

"This is as Goth as it gets. Try it."

I took the harp with both hands.

The shopkeeper hurried over with a folding chair.

"Oh—thank you." All the attention felt strange. I sat and positioned the harp in my lap. "Where do your hands go?"

The shopkeeper leaned in. "Here, and here. Right hand treble, left hand bass."

"Where is middle C?"

She pointed to a red string in the middle of the harp.

I hummed "Good King Wenceslas" to refresh my memory. Then I picked it out on the harp—slowly, one note at a time.

Oliver beamed. "You play by ear!" His proximity carried with it a fresh touch of bergamot over the woody fragrance I'd noticed before.

The scent mingled with the aroma of the Christmas market as I continued plucking the harp strings. I shook my head. "I don't play at all."

"But you could," said the shopkeeper. "Imagine sitting by the fire with your very own harp." Her hopeful smile conjured the scene.

Elegant little Gothic harps and medieval melodies danced through my head, followed by a vivid image of Oliver and I beside a roaring fire. A strange but pleasant sense of relaxation stole through me—which I cut off by returning the harp to its stand. I stood up. "I'll think about it," I said, by which I meant I would firmly shove it out of my mind as soon as possible. I treated myself to small things, like nail polish and lipstick, not wildly impractical and expensive musical instruments.

Still, I couldn't resist a backwards glance after we left the booth and continued down the aisle.

"So, your nieces think you're Goth?"

I chuckled, remembering the morning's mini-makeover. "Something like that."

"Christmas is very Goth."

"You're joking."

"I'm quite serious. It's the coldest, darkest time of the year. So dark and depressing that we drag a tree into the house and set it on fire just to stave off the sadness." He waved his hand, as if to conjure a tree. "Goth."

I laughed. "I think most people would prefer not to set it on fire." I thought of Horatio, and hoped he would not get any ideas about setting trees on fire.

We arrived at the booth selling wax paper packets of roasted nuts coated in sugar and cinnamon.

"One, please," I said to the vendor. I held out cash, preempting Oliver before he had a chance to offer to pay.

He made a face at being thwarted, then ordered a packet for himself.

We continued walking down the next aisle of the Christmas market.

"You cannot prevent me from fulfilling my obligation so easily," he said. "I shall insist on purchasing your choice of hot chocolate, cider, tea, or coffee."

I stopped in the middle of the aisle. "Look, Oliver, I don't want you to get the wrong idea."

He arched his eyebrows.

"I'm truly sorry I kissed you the other day—no, that came out wrong. I was only thinking of one thing—"

His eyebrows climbed even higher.

"God, I'm making a mess of this." I pressed my hand to my forehead. "I shouldn't have roped you into chasing your boss. I put you in a sticky situation that could have gotten you in trouble. What I'm trying to say is: I'm sorry."

"Say no more, my dear Rose. Your company is all the restitution I could ask for."

My brain got stuck on *my dear Rose* and spun in circles like an animated download hourglass. Why did he have to talk like an old romance novel? Not that I ever read romance novels.

Well, not recently, anyway.

"Besides," he continued, "I am as curious about her activities as you are. It's not like her to take meetings alone in abandoned warehouses. I may be her employee, but I confess that her welfare concerns me; during my time in her service, I have grown fond of her—" His gaze caught my facial expression. "Are you surprised?"

I hesitated, searching for the right words. "She seems ..."

"A tough nut to crack?" Oliver smiled and tossed a nut into the air, catching it in his mouth.

"You could say that," I replied, with all the diplomatic neutrality I could manage. She also had an unfortunate habit of hypnotizing people and tossing them off lighthouses, but I couldn't share that small character flaw with Oliver. "How do you suggest we keep an eye on her?"

"Perhaps we could work together."

Did he mean *work* together, or did he want to spend more time with me for other reasons? Never had I been so tempted to put my fledgling mind reading skills to use. Mrs. Millefleur had told me to practice, hadn't she?

But it would be wrong to read his private thoughts ... unless I was very careful and only read the most pertinent, surface thoughts.

I couldn't stop myself. I reached out with my magic and traced the edge of his consciousness.

Before I could even find the contours of his mental landscape, let alone make anything out, Oliver tripped—spectacularly. The paper packet went flying, and the toasted nuts scattered across the walkway and the nearby tables with a clatter.

He landed hard on the ground.

I dropped to my knees beside him. "Oliver! Are you okay?"

He winced. When he lifted his hands, the gravel had left red indentations on his palms. "I believe I've sprained my dignity."

Guilt surged through me. I helped him sit up, then brushed at his clothes to remove the grit. "I'm so sorry—"

"Why? You did nothing wrong. It was my own clumsy feet." He wiggled his perfectly polished loafers as if to prove the point. "Too bad about the nuts, though." He looked around with a forlorn expression. The cinnamon-sugared treats were scattered in all directions.

I pressed my own warm packet of spiced nuts into his hands. "Here. You can have mine."

Our fingers touched, and he looked into my eyes. "Perhaps I should trip more often."

14

Luella insisted I swing by Pepper's house before I picked up my dog training client that afternoon. She had something for me but refused to tell me what it was, instead insisting that I would find out soon enough.

When I arrived, Pepper met me at the door. The sunlight streaming in lit up the lustrous black pearl on her leather necklace. "Come on through."

I followed her through the house to where she and Luella had been hanging out by the pool.

Pepper picked up a chair from the other end of the pool area and hauled it over. She dropped it next to Luella's and returned to her own seat. "Sit. Spill," she said.

I sat, but gave her a pointed look. "I am not a dog."

Pepper grinned, unabashed. "Good Rose." Tiny globes of water rose from the pool and drifted in my direction.

I ignited my fingertips and intercepted the globes, blasting them into tiny clouds of steam.

Luella waved a hand. A gust of wind dispersed the steam. "Rose, you're stalling."

"I'm not stalling."

"You're obviously uncomfortable. Pepper, doesn't she look uncomfortable?"

Pepper squinted in my direction. "Fast heartbeat."

I rolled my eyes. "Oh, great, now you're reading people's moods, too."

"You'd feel better if you just told us everything that happened," said Luella.

So I did, from seeing Oliver under the palm tree to his sudden fall in the Christmas market.

Pepper's mouth fell open. "You read his mind?"

I covered my face with my hands. "For God's sake, Pepper, you don't need to shout. And no, I didn't."

"You tried to," Luella pointed out unhelpfully.

"How else was I supposed to know his motivations?"

Luella made a face. "I don't know—maybe *talk* to him?"

"I wanted to be sure."

"Why don't you just admit you like the guy?" asked Pepper. "Hell, you already kissed him—and you liked that."

"I—he's nice, I guess."

"You guess? You *guess*?" Pepper shook her head. "You're hopeless."

Luella shook her head. "She's nervous."

"You're nervous?" said Pepper. "Why?"

"I'm not—" I stopped, aware that lying to my friends was not only wrong, it was pointless, too, because they'd see right through it. "Maybe I am a little nervous. It was hard seeing what my mom went through when my dad left. And now look at my sister …"

"You're not getting married, Rose," said Luella, gently. "You can walk away at any time. And it's okay to have fun. Give yourself permission to have fun."

"But if he gives you any trouble, we know where the good swamps are," added Pepper. "The ones with extra gators."

I laughed. Weight lifted off my chest that I hadn't even known I was carrying. "Between the permission to have fun, and the promise to hide the body if I don't, you two have pretty much solved all my problems, haven't you?" I leaned back in the chair and tilted my face to the sun. "Anyway, we agreed to stay in touch, and to meet up and compare notes periodically."

"If you have to call it 'comparing notes' to feel comfortable going on a date, I'm down with that," said Pepper.

"It's not a date," I said.

"But does *he* think it's a date?"

"How should I know?"

"Easy," Pepper said. "Read his mind."

Luella shook her head. "You don't need to read his mind to know he's interested in you. Of course he is. He wouldn't be wandering around Christmas markets with you otherwise."

"I'll try to save the mind reading for emergencies."

Pepper framed a rectangular shape with her hands. "Mind reading: Break glass in case of emergency." Then she propped her hands behind her head in a thoughtful pose. "Yeah, no one wants you to go full Millefleur."

"No danger of that," said Luella. "Rose is a paragon of morality."

"Am I?"

They looked at me.

I held my hands up in a placating gesture. "I'm kidding. Of course I'm not going to go 'full Millefleur.'"

We all went quiet for a moment. The sound of the pool fountain filled the gap in the conversation.

I sighed. "I better get going. I have to pick up a dog for agility training." Reluctance to leave made me slow to stand. Sitting by the pool appealed a lot more than work, even if work was training an adorable Chihuahua to run up a ramp.

"Hang on." Luella rummaged in her purse. "I almost forgot why I asked you to swing by—I got you an early Christmas present."

"You didn't have to do that—"

"Hush." She pulled out an envelope. "Here."

I took the envelope and peeked inside. It held a neat stack of tickets. I drew one out and read it aloud. "Circus Aetherium: Admit One." I hugged Luella. "You didn't have to do that."

She hugged me back. "I knew you all wanted to go. But there's something else, too—a little surprise at the show—and you have to promise me you won't freak out, no matter what happens."

"You know surprises make me anxious, Luella—can't you just tell me ahead of time?"

"No, but everybody's going—me, Mama, Raphael, Pepper and her family—and it'll be a fun surprise, I promise."

I'd have rather died than let Luella think I was ungrateful for her kind gift, so I smiled and thanked her, adding that my nieces would be over the moon.

Pepper walked me out. "We sure didn't practice much."

"Next time," I said. "We'll practice next time."

On the doorstep, Pepper paused. "Hey." She landed a single, lightweight punch on my arm. "We know you're not going to the dark side, Rose. We're just teasing you." She cocked her head. "You know that, right?"

I don't know what flickered over my face in that moment, but whatever it was, it made Pepper pull me in for an unexpected hug. "What was that for?"

"Because you needed it," she said, with matter-of-fact cheer. "Now go get that little doggy and get to work."

The door clicked shut as I blinked in the harsh sunlight.

For once, I didn't summon Horatio to accompany me on the drive. I wasn't sure how my doggy client would react to a magical cat in the cab—better to err on the side of caution. Hopefully, Horatio wouldn't take it into his head to pop in unexpectedly.

I headed to another neighborhood to collect Peanut, the formerly nervous Chihuahua, from his owner. With Peanut buckled securely into the harness I'd set up in the front seat, I pointed the truck toward home. "How are you today, Peanut?"

Peanut shook his head vigorously, which made his tufted ears flap.

"Have you been a good boy lately?"

His little tongue popped out.

"I'll take that as a yes. You're making friends with all the other dogs, right? Not getting scared, and barking, and running away?"

Peanut's face stretched into a doggy grin.

"That's good. It's hard to learn to trust. You're doing great, by the way." At a stoplight, I patted his round little caramel-colored head. "Today we get to play on the agility course. You'll like that. I'll teach you some new skills to impress all your friends."

At the cabin, I attached a leash to his collar and walked him up to the door. I opened the door a crack and peeked in.

Braveheart, keen to the sound of the key in the lock, had already trotted into the living room.

"Braveheart, sit."

He sat.

"Come on, Peanut. Say hello to Braveheart." I led the smaller dog inside.

Peanut flinched, then recovered.

That deserved a reward—Braveheart could be intimidating. I knelt and gave Peanut a thorough pat along with heaps of verbal praise.

I led the Chihuahua down the hall and stopped at the guest bedroom to find Izzy, Astrid, and Sadie piled on the bed watching an animated movie on the small television. A neat row of bags indicated they'd already finished packing. "I'm taking Peanut on the agility course."

Sadie bounced up. "Can we watch?"

I glanced at my sister. "I don't want to interrupt your movie time ..."

"I wouldn't miss this," said Izzy. She swung her legs over the side of the bed and sat up. "Astrid?"

Astrid stretched, then swept back her black-and-green hair. "I'm in."

They followed us outside and took seats at the picnic table.

I ran Peanut through his obedience commands—sit, stay, come, heel, and lie down—to get him warmed up. I chose one of the less intimidating obstacles to introduce Peanut to my backyard agility course. The A-frame, a simple but steep ramp, would require Peanut to walk up one side and down the other.

I led him quickly to the ramp so he wouldn't have time to overthink it, but at the incline, he balked.

"You can do it, Peanut!" Sadie cheered from the sideline.

I walked him away from the obstacle, then looped back.

No dice. Peanut stopped at the bottom of the ramp, then shied back a few steps.

I palmed a dog treat from my pocket. Lucky for me, a tiny Chihuahua like Peanut was easy to lift. I picked him up and placed him on the down ramp, two or three steps from the bottom. The treat rewarded him for taking those last few steps off the ramp.

We walked back to the other side of the ramp.

Peanut regarded the incline. He cocked his head with a dubious expression.

I palmed another treat and showed it to him.

His tufted ears perked. With the treat in front of him, he took one step, then another, then another, all the way up the ramp. At the top he seemed to suddenly recall he was doing something out of the ordinary—but the treat caught his attention and he followed it the rest of the way down.

I fed him the treat as soon as all four paws touched the ground. "Good boy, Peanut! What a brave doggy you are!"

Izzy, Sadie, and Astrid cheered.

"You see, Peanut? Not everything unfamiliar is dangerous." My gaze drifted over the obstacle course, and the reverse of the reassurance rang dissonantly in my mind: *Not everything dangerous is unfamiliar.*

15

Izzy and I planned to leave the cabin at the exact same time to ensure we arrived at her house simultaneously. The kids had been told that I had to clear out of the cabin while a complex plumbing problem was resolved. While it wasn't the most convincing ruse ever, it was good enough to hold up under mild scrutiny—and even if Damon suspected I was there for some other reason, he wouldn't be able to do a thing about it.

Although Izzy knew I planned to run interference between her and Damon, I hadn't revealed my plans to get him to leave the house of his own volition. Nor had I mentioned that I would be using magic to do it.

Nervous energy made me rub my arms, though it wasn't that cold. I massaged the muscles of my upper arms in an attempt to loosen the tightness. The sensation made me remember the pain of adding the leaves of fire to my rose tattoo.

Izzy, Astrid, and Sadie slammed their car doors.

It was time to go. I checked Braveheart's safety harness one more time—he was much larger than Peanut, but I'd adjusted the harness after dropping off the little Chihuahua.

Our small caravan rolled out of the woods and away from the cabin I called home.

I summoned my other furry ally.

Horatio popped into being with a flash, landing on the narrow middle seat rather than his usual shotgun seat, which was occupied by Braveheart.

Braveheart took Horatio's sudden appearance in stride, being thoroughly used to the black cat's abrupt comings and goings.

We drove the short distance to Izzy's house. I parked along the street, turned off the truck, and paused to crack my knuckles. Izzy and the girls were already bustling up the front walk to the door. I regarded Braveheart and Horatio. "You ready, my friends?"

Braveheart's tongue lolled. He was probably more ready to make friends than make trouble.

Horatio set his claws into my leg and stretched.

I absorbed the points of pain without flinching. I could handle worse.

I got out of the truck, freed Braveheart from the harness, and attached a leash before I followed Izzy and the girls up the driveway. Horatio followed behind. I caught the front door just as it was swinging closed.

Damon stood in the living room. He did a double-take as I entered the room. "What is *she* doing here?"

Astrid fielded the question with a tone somewhere between wide-eyed sincerity and sarcastic amusement. "Aunt Rose is having plumbing problems."

Damon shot me a confused look.

I leveled a stare at him and didn't say a word.

"But...why the dog?"

Sadie placed her arms around Braveheart's substantial neck. "He's sleeping over!"

Damon's gaze traveled from the dog to me. He was an arrogant snake, but he wasn't entirely stupid. The realization that I was there for some other reason played over his face as obviously as a flashing sign.

My smile said: *You're recalculating your plans, now, aren't you, you little bastard.* A rush of adrenalin seized me.

He blinked. "There's no space for your sister—"

"She can bunk with me," said Izzy.

Faced with sisterly solidarity, Damon muttered something about taking a shower and retreated down the hallway.

Izzy covered her mouth to suppress a laugh.

I wanted to celebrate the small victory, but I had work to do if Damon was getting in the shower. "Izzy, can I rest in your room for a little while?"

"Knock yourself out."

I hurried to the bedroom and closed the door, then pulled off my boots and lay down.

Horatio jumped onto the bed and curled up on my belly.

I closed my eyes and magic surged through my veins like silver lightning. My stomach trembled. I sought the sources of heat in the house, discarding them one by one until I found the one I wanted.

The shower.

After the failed attempt to put out the fire in the cabin fireplace, I'd practiced. I started with a candle and put it out over and over again. Then I worked on cooling liquids until I could chill a cup of coffee with a thought.

It was tricky to hone in on the pipe carrying hot water, but I did it. With my eyes squeezed shut, I reached with my mind and wrapped my magic around the pipe. I drew the heat out as fast as it poured in.

Horatio stirred. His tail brightened from a candle flame to a concentrated spark like an acetylene torch, bright enough to be seen through my closed eyelids.

A muffled shriek and a thumping scramble carried through the walls from the direction of the bathroom.

I released the heat and waited. The water turned off and on again, striking the tub with a hollow sound. When the sound mellowed, I knew Damon had climbed in again—trusting that the ice-cold water had been a fluke.

I resolved to do it even faster. The water pulsed through the pipe: hot, hot, hot, hot—cold! All in one burst I yanked the heat away. It must have been close to freezing, for Damon yelped like he'd been whipped. My heart thumped with joy. I sank my fingers into Horatio's fur and murmured praise.

The bathroom door banged open. Damon's voice rang in the hallway. "There's something wrong with the hot water." He stomped away in the direction of the hot water heater.

I chuckled—but the mirth died on my lips. I had forgotten to take Izzy into account. My purpose was to make *Damon* think the house was falling apart, not worry my sister to death.

I pressed my hands to my forehead. This was a conundrum.

Horatio let out a questioning meow.

I scratched his head. "I'm going to have to tell her, Horatio. No two ways about it." I sat up, shifting the cat onto my lap. "Izzy?" I called. "Can you come here for a sec?"

Moments later, the doorknob turned, and Izzy came in. The wrinkles between her eyebrows looked deeper than ever. "Damon said the hot water heater's broken."

"About that …" I patted the bed. "Sit down."

Her eyebrows rose, making the wrinkles disappear. She sat next to me on the bed. "I'm not sure I like conversations that start with 'sit down.'"

I reached for her hands—and then she really looked nervous.

"Rose, did someone die?"

"No one died."

Izzy exhaled. "Thank God. I can't take any more bad news."

"This isn't bad news." I paused. This wasn't easy. "You know how you're always telling the girls they each have their own gifts?"

She nodded slowly.

"Well, it turns out that I have a gift of my own." Now that it was time for the truth to come out, the words were elusive. I soldiered on. "It turns out, apparently, that some people have abilities exceeding what you might consider to be normal."

Izzy shifted. The look on her face changed from benign interest to sisterly concern. "Rose—"

This wasn't working at all. I shook my head. "It's easier to show you."

"Show me what?"

"Hand me one of those receipts. Make sure it's one you don't need."

She snagged a receipt from the pile on her dresser and handed it to me.

"You don't need this, do you?" After she shook her head, I continued. "Promise me you won't freak out, okay? Don't scream."

Izzy frowned. "Why would I—"

I held the receipt out, conjured silver fire to the tip of my finger, and touched the paper. It ignited. Izzy gasped, but I cut her off with a shushing sound. With the receipt half-burned, I clenched my other hand into a fist and made the fire go out without touching it.

"How did you—"

"Magic."

She made a skeptical face and leaned back on her hands. "You're tricking me."

"No tricks. I promise."

She grabbed my hands and turned them over, looking for clues.

"Look all you want."

Izzy released my hands, grabbed another receipt, and held it out. "Do it again."

I looked at the receipt. "This is for potted plants. You sure you don't want to save this one in case you kill them and want to cash in on the guarantee?"

She slapped my arm. "I never kill plants. That's your specialty. Now get on with it."

I ignited the home improvement store receipt, then extinguished it before it burned too close to my fingers.

"Show me something else."

What else could I show her? I looked around the room. I could burn things all day long if she wanted me to—but what I really wanted to show her was Horatio. "I actually have a magical cat that helps me. He's right here"—I pointed to my lap—"but he's invisible to anyone who isn't magical."

Izzy stood up in an abrupt motion. "That's ridiculous—"

"Sit down. I'll prove it." On second thought, how would I prove it? Izzy wasn't magical. Horatio could set something on fire, but that wouldn't make him visible to her. I racked my brain. Surely there was something I could do.

Would hypnosis work?

I snapped my fingers. "Let's try this. Sit facing me."

She angled herself in my direction. Judging by the look on her face, she was reluctant to indulge me in what appeared to be madness.

"I'm going to suggest that you can see him—"

"Suggest?"

"Like hypnosis."

"Oh, so you have magical hypnosis powers, too?"

"That's part of it." If this didn't work, I didn't know what I would do. "You want to see him, right?"

"Of course I want to see your imaginary magical cat."

The desire was there. I could work with that. I concentrated on what I could see—namely, Horatio—and willed Izzy to see him, too. "Look. Right here." I patted Horatio and prayed it didn't look like I was patting empty air. "He's right in front of you."

She squinted. Her irises flickered silver.

I willed the magic to hold, that she would see Horatio with her own eyes.

Her mouth dropped open. "He's—he's there! On your lap! Why couldn't I see him before?" She stretched out her hand in wonderment. "Can I touch him?"

"You can try." I concentrated on the sensation of Horatio's fur, hoping it would be as warm and real under her fingers as it was under mine. Sweat broke out on my brow.

She lowered her hand to Horatio's shoulders. Her fingers sank into his fur.

Our eyes met—and I knew she believed.

16

As much as I wanted to hold on to the moment—to share Horatio with Izzy as long as possible—a wave of dizziness washed over me.

I broke the connection. I couldn't risk losing control of my powers.

"Where'd he go?" said Izzy.

"He's still there."

Her shoulders slumped. "I wish I could see him all the time." She eyed me speculatively. "Did you have something to do with Damon running out of the shower?"

I did my very best impression of a woman of mystery.

Izzy punched my shoulder. "There's nothing wrong with the water heater, is there? You did that!"

I burst out laughing.

She laughed, too. After I related what really happened when I went to get Astrid and Sadie's things, we giggled helplessly until we both fell over on the bed, gasping for breath.

"I needed that," said Izzy. She sighed with deep satisfaction before continuing. "So what else are you going to do?"

"Whatever I can come up with. By the time I get done with him, he'll think the house is a money pit. He won't be able to leave fast enough."

"You really think you can do that?"

"I think I can. We'll get some help, too."

"Help?"

I had to go all the way back to the beginning and tell her the full story of the Ride-or-Die Witches—after swearing her to secrecy.

"I can't believe all this is real," she said.

"It's real."

She pushed herself up to a sitting position. "Do you think I could get some magical powers of my own?"

I blinked. "I have no idea. This is all pretty new to me."

Izzy toyed with the stacks of bangles on her wrists.

"What are you thinking about?"

Mischief sparked in her eyes. "I'm imagining everything I could do with magical powers."

I would have split my magic in half and handed it to her if I knew how. Instead, I sat up and put an arm around her shoulder. "Whatever you can imagine, I can do. We're a team."

She held up a hand in a signal for silence, then cocked her head. "I think I hear Damon in the kitchen."

We stood and moved to the door to listen.

"He's cooking," she said. "I hear the pots and pans."

"You think I should wreck his culinary ambitions?"

She clapped a hand on my bicep and gave me a little shake. "You bet your tattoo, I do."

I closed my eyes and prepared to zap the heat from the burners.

"Wait," said Izzy. "I want to watch his reaction."

"You don't think he'll get suspicious?"

"Just this once. Please?"

I weighed the risk of Damon catching on against how happy it would make Izzy to see him confounded. Izzy's happiness won. "All right. But be cool, okay?"

Izzy opened the door and led the way into the living room, which faced the kitchen across a bar. She looked almost *too* casual as she flopped on the couch, picked up a magazine, and began leafing through the pages.

Luckily, Damon wasn't paying that much attention.

I settled on the couch and turned on the TV—it would give me an excuse to sit and stare in one direction, for concentration purposes, without looking odd.

A local newscaster burbled on about the best local Christmas decorations, but I tuned him out and allowed my focus to drift into another level of reality.

The heat of the burner element appeared in my awareness like a frisbee of red light. I closed a web of magic over it. Then I waited. The burner was far hotter than the water in the shower pipe, and took longer to master. Several minutes ticked by while I drained the heat from the element.

Damon lifted the pot and cursed. He switched off the first burner and moved the pot to another burner.

I shifted the web to the second burner and smiled. I could do this all day.

Damon hovered over the stove. Again, nothing happened. His curses became more dire as he moved the pot to a third burner.

Izzy had a look of amusement on her face. "A watched pot never boils."

Damon pivoted in her direction. "You know what, Isabella? You can just—" His gaze shifted to me and he caught himself. His voice ratcheted down from rude to bewildered. He tried the fourth burner. "I just don't understand what's wrong with this thing. The light comes on, but the burner doesn't get hot."

"Time for a new stove," said Izzy, affecting a doleful tone. Out of sight of Damon, she gave me a wink and a thumbs-up.

I almost snorted.

Damon abandoned the pot and left the room. He returned wearing a jacket and carrying his keys. Without another word, he flounced out the front door.

Izzy and I ran to the window to watch him leave.

"He'll go buy himself lunch," she said.

"He sure didn't try too hard with the stove."

She smirked. "Persistence isn't his strong point."

"That's a less than generous observation, Izzy. I'm proud of you."

A sweet voice piped up from behind us. "What're you looking at?"

"The weather," said Izzy without missing a beat.

My sister, the world-class fibber.

Sadie joined us at the window. "Is it going to snow?" She put her face so close to the glass it pressed her nose flat.

Izzy smoothed Sadie's hair. "No, angel. It doesn't get that cold in Florida."

"Where did Daddy go?"

Izzy's gaze met mine before shifting to her daughter. "The stove didn't work, so I think he went out to eat."

Sadie turned away from the window. "He won't bring us any. He never does."

Even though Sadie's delivery was matter-of-fact, Izzy flinched. "Why don't I make you something?"

"But the stove doesn't work—"

Izzy hustled Sadie into the kitchen. "Let's see if Mommy can make it work." She rummaged in the cabinet and pulled out a blue box. "How does macaroni and cheese sound?"

"Yay! Macaroni and cheese!"

"Ask your sister if she wants some."

Sadie ran off.

I leaned over the bar. "He doesn't bring them anything when he treats himself?"

"It doesn't occur to him to consider anyone else's needs."

It was my turn to flinch. My clients had more consideration for their dogs than my brother-in-law did for his family.

Izzy held up a second blue box. "You want some mac and cheese?"

I shook myself to chase away the dark thoughts. "Pass. I'm taking Braveheart out."

Braveheart, loyal and easygoing dog that he was, seemed perfectly in tune with my need to get out of the house. My sister's neighborhood bordered the same sprawling forest—Black Bear Ridge—that marked the end of my backyard miles away. I walked Braveheart toward the end of the development.

I summoned Horatio. He manifested on my shoulders like a furry stole.

The three of us approached the unfenced border between the neighborhood and the forest. When we crossed into the forest, the sounds of traffic and the whirr of heating units fell away. I didn't want to go far enough in to risk getting lost, just far enough to feel like I'd left the world behind me for a few peaceful moments.

I cast my awareness into the air and pushed it outward. Small bundles of heat criss-crossed the pine branches, while others darted in fits and starts across the pine needle-covered ground.

Braveheart sniffed the ground—which gave me an idea.

I pushed the magic into the earth and felt the depth of the cold sand. Below it, something else entirely: a lake—no, an *ocean* of water—under my feet.

It was one thing to know of the existence of the aquifer, another thing altogether to sense the land resting on it like a raft. Desirable Sparkle Beach condo units cost hundreds of thousands for their spectacular river views, and yet even the humblest mainland home could be considered waterfront property if you turned your perspective sideways.

Sometimes, perspective made all the difference.

Which one was truly more desirable, Izzy's house or a glittering condominium tower? I knew what Izzy would answer. She'd poured her love and the work of her own hands into one earnest project after another, from cheerful paint jobs to xeriscaping and handmade windchimes.

But what about Damon?

The phone in my back pocket buzzed, interrupting my train of thought. The bubble of magic dissipated. "Isn't that always the way?" I pulled out the phone as it continued to buzz.

Not a text, then. A call.

Oliver.

"Hello?"

"Sorry to bother you, dear Rose, but do you have a moment?"

I smiled as I fanned the flames of a new idea. "I'm glad you called. I need to ask you a favor."

17

I glanced at my nails one more time. The designs I'd applied were fresh, and I worried they were still soft. The lacquer glinted in the disorienting multicolored spotlights over the bar.

I forced my hands down and scanned the crowd. Why had I suggested Oliver and I meet at my old stomping grounds? I hadn't been to Lovecats in years.

Decades.

It was a miracle it hadn't ceased to exist.

The club had abandoned the familiar music of my youth. The new music struck my ear like echoes from the future—not bad, by any means—but its very newness reminded me of the passage of time with every beat.

I could handle a little *memento mori*. If anything, it sharpened my purpose like steel on stone. This meeting with Oliver, in addition to providing me with a certain something I needed, gave me the opportunity to see Oliver out of his element. Shaken up. Surprised. To hell with cute coffee shops and charming Christmas markets—toss him into a dark club, and maybe I'd get to see who he really was outside of his polished chauffeur persona.

I expected he would show up in one of his work suits, or in the sweater and tweed combo he'd worn at our last meetup, looking wildly out of place.

I was wrong. God, was I ever wrong.

He wore black—and he wore it well. A tailored black overcoat worn like armor against the wind that chased through the door as it swung closed behind him. The sea of young people parted and gave way. He closed the distance between us.

A smile lifted the corners of his lips as he made eye contact and pulled off his black leather gloves. "Is this what you wanted?"

My mouth went dry, and my vocabulary—so prolific at other times—deserted me.

He reached for an inner jacket pocket and fanned a stack of glossy brochures on the bar in a smooth magician's pass.

I pulled my gaze away from his face and blinked at the array. "Yes. Yes, that was exactly what I wanted."

He settled gracefully on the barstool next to me and signaled the bartender. "Black Velvet, please. Rose?"

I was still staring at the brochures. "Diet Coke and red wine."

Oliver tapped the glossy paper. "Care to tell me what this is all about? Are you making a killing in the real estate market?"

The bass-heavy music pulsed through me. I swept the brochures into a stack and tucked them into my bag. To buy time to organize my thoughts, I drank from the glass the bartender had silently delivered. "My brother-in-law is having a midlife crisis. The brochures are breadcrumbs to lead him away from my sister."

"Do tell."

I eyed him, gauging his sincerity. The illumination played tricks with light and shadow, casting his face half in darkness, half in streaks of color. In my peripheral vision, bodies gyrated on the dance floor. "They're getting a divorce. I want to convince him that he'd be happier if he moved out and let my sister keep the house."

"Your sister would be happier, to be sure."

I acknowledged the truth with a nod, expecting a look of judgment.

Oliver's eyebrows lifted, but instead of judgment, a wicked smile indicated approval. "Devious. But surely a few brochures won't be enough to make up his mind ... unless you have more in mind."

"Oh, there's more."

"Of course there is." He drank from his glass. "I must say, dear Rose—I like the way you operate."

"Thank you." Between the compliment, the *dear Rose*, and his black ensemble, I struggled to focus on what I'd come for. Was it the brochures? Was it to find out more about Oliver? An impulse to flee overtook me. I glanced over my shoulder, toward the door.

Only a few steps across the room and I'd be free of this confusion.

Oliver spoke, drawing my attention. "If it were me …"

"Yes?"

He set down his glass and gave me a frank look. "If it were me, I would make his current situation untenable in addition to tempting him with a glamorous bachelor pad of his very own."

I smirked. "If only you knew."

"If I don't know, then tell me."

"I can't."

"Are you afraid I won't keep your secrets?"

"I don't even know you."

"Then get to know me."

I laughed. "I know you like Black Velvets. That you drive a Lincoln Town Car for a living. That you're a snazzy dresser."

"I'm blushing—but you didn't even mention my accent."

"It speaks for itself."

"Touché." He leaned on the bar. "What else do you want to know?"

"What do you know about me?"

He smiled at the challenge. "I know you drink a very odd concoction"—he eyed my glass—"and that you favor the color black. You have an ear for music. Your fingernails are emblazoned with a dagger, a flame, two pawprints, and a crescent moon. And you kissed me in the rain."

I inhaled carefully. Air seemed in short supply. Despite the cold winter night, the air inside the bar was close and heavy. I cleared my throat. "What else would you like to know?"

"Everything."

I looked away from his magnetic gaze, and tried to laugh off the warmth that was spreading across my skin. "We'd be here all night."

"I have no objections."

Whatever crackled between us felt like falling out of an airplane. I couldn't sit there any longer. I tossed back the rest of my drink. "Let's dance." I stood and didn't look back to see if he followed me to the dance floor.

The beat dropped and I let it roll through me.

No more words—only music and motion.

We found our rhythm together. The music drowned out anything but the impulse to *feel, feel, feel*, and in the flashing lights we were neither young nor old, with no history and no future but the now. I reached for Oliver, and the sensation of falling changed to one of flying.

Temptation roiled me. It would take only the lightest brush to know his thoughts. My magic floated in the air between us like silver smoke. I hesitated—he didn't know what I could do, didn't have a way to guard himself, *it would be wrong*—

And then he kissed me.

Right there on the dance floor, under the disorienting lights, he swept me into his arms and kissed me. Coherent thought burned to a crisp as the sensation overwhelmed every synapse. It was as if my own magic had been turned back on me, and instead of knowing Oliver's thoughts, I'd been plunged into my own.

My breath caught. Embers of emotions I thought I'd smothered long ago roared to life, and the intensity rocked me harder than the thumping bass.

Where had the air gone when I needed it?

"Outside," I said, with my lips close to his ear.

He followed me without a word.

We burst through the door of the club into the cold air. The constellation Orion blazed in a cloudless night sky. We walked a distance from the club, the loud music receding into the distance, before I stopped and faced him.

"I need to be straight with you."

"Be my guest."

My sigh condensed in the moonlight. "I'm no one's girlfriend, Oliver."

"I wouldn't have kissed you if you were."

"That's not what I mean."

He cocked his head. "My dear Rose," he said. "You're adorable."

"I am not adorable. I live alone with my dog and I like it that way. I'm not interested in being tied down—"

"Heaven forbid," he said.

I shot him a look. "So I don't want you to get the wrong idea or anything."

He regarded me with a solemn look. It didn't take a mind-reader to see that it was entirely bogus.

"Go ahead, smirk your little smirk."

"I would never."

"I see it." I stared him down. "Right there at the corner of your lip."

He touched his lips. "Here?"

I had miscalculated. Now that my attention was back on his lips, I wanted to kiss him again. Or possibly smack him.

I wasn't sure which.

18

I paid the price for staying up long past my bedtime. My head ached as I dragged myself to Izzy's kitchen for coffee—only to find Damon monopolizing the machine.

He fiddled with the filter and the grounds, then closed the basket and toggled the switch.

Tired as I was, it took barely any effort to drain the warmth from the coffeemaker's internal heating element.

Damon slapped the machine, reopened the basket and the lid, then shut everything again.

Of course, nothing happened. "Maybe there's something wrong with the electricity, if all these appliances are malfunctioning," I said, helpfully-but-not-so-helpfully.

"Like you would know," he replied.

I shrugged and did my best to look innocent.

He stormed off and slammed the bathroom door.

I released my magical hold on the coffee machine. When Damon turned on the shower, I waited for him to get in—I could tell by the change in the sound of the water hitting the tub—then hijacked the heat in one sharp jerk.

Damon yelled several choice obscenities.

Izzy entered the kitchen and patted my back. "I see you've been busy this morning."

"Tell him you had to take a cold shower, too." I restarted the coffeemaker. The cheerful brewing noise sounded like victory; I was definitely getting better at manipulating heat. When the coffeemaker finished brewing, I poured a full cup for my sister and one for myself. "Damon is off today, right?"

Izzy nodded and took a careful sip of the hot coffee.

"I'm calling in to Suntan Queen. Going to have a few friends over."

"While Damon's here?"

"We have ... plans."

"Oh, *plans*." Her eyes widened. "I like the sound of that."

"Now you get yourself to work, and the kids to school, and don't worry about a thing."

She saluted me. "Yes, ma'am, Your Roseness."

I waited until she'd left the kitchen before I pulled out my phone. I started a new group text with Luella and Pepper, looping in Raphael. *You guys ready to roll? Come prepared with your best ideas.*

Are you still up for this, considering you stayed up past your beddy-bye time? asked Pepper.

LOL Pepper, you're hilarious, I replied.

She sent back an emoji face with its tongue sticking out.

I pocketed my phone. By the time I finished my coffee, Izzy and the girls had left. Damon remained in his room. It was the perfect time to plant the real estate brochures.

I summoned Horatio, gave him a cuddle and a scratch, then allowed him to ride on my shoulders as I moved about the house. I left condo brochures tucked here and there. Each was more tempting than the last. I opened the last remaining brochure and flipped through the pages. *Luxury, location, life. Capture the feeling!* Heavily oiled women in bathing suits draped themselves over pool furniture while bare-chested men raised colorful mixed drinks with tiny paper umbrellas.

Capture the feeling, indeed. Pure midlife crisis bait. It was the best hard sell of the bunch, so I put it in the bathroom where I knew he would see it.

I retreated to Izzy's room with a notebook and a pad of paper to brainstorm. There wouldn't be unlimited chances to make magical mischief with my friends, so I needed to make the most of having free rein while Damon was home but everyone else was not.

I was running out of heat-related appliances to put on the fritz. How could my friends up the ante? Pepper had already suggested blasting Damon with toilet water. Luella wasn't sure what she could do, but I had an inkling that if she and I worked together, we could surround him with drafts of cold air. Raphael's powers were somewhat limited—not to mention harder to control—but he was game to try whatever we could come up with.

That covered appliances, electrical problems, plumbing, and possibly heating and air-conditioning issues, if Luella and I could get that to work. I tore the page of notes out of the notebook. I didn't need to keep it—the act of writing by hand was enough to get my brain working—so I crumpled the page and placed it in a bowl. One touch, and the paper burned to ashes.

Horatio jumped down and stuck his nose in the bowl, then shook his head so hard his ears flapped.

"Did you get ashes on your little kitty nose?"

He stalked away in silent indignation.

I cleaned up, walked Braveheart, and had just settled down with a book to kill time when someone knocked on the door. "Luella," I said to myself. "Always early."

I opened the door to find Luella and Raphael standing on the doorstep wearing matching knitted ski hats with pom-poms. "You two are disgusting."

"Thank you," said Raphael as they stepped inside.

Luella laughed. She pulled off her hat and fluffed her hair. "You're one to talk, Rose."

"Oh?" said Raphael. His gaze traveled from Luella to me. "Did I miss something?"

"Nope." I wasn't ready to talk about Oliver with anyone but my closest friends and Izzy.

Luella put her arm around my shoulder and gave me a squeeze that combined a hug and a shake. Then she sat on the couch. "Where's—"

"Down the hall," I said.

Raphael spoke quietly. "What's the plan?"

"Play it by ear. I don't know what he'll be doing, so we'll have to figure it out as we go."

A pounding noise came from the front door. It sounded like someone was trying to kick the door down.

"It's me!" said Pepper from outside. "My hands are full."

I jogged to the door and pulled it open.

Pepper brandished large bags that smelled of Chinese food. "Lunch!"

I ushered her in and helped her unload the containers onto the bar.

"So where is the bastard?" said Pepper, seemingly unconcerned about the bastard in question overhearing her. She dug into a container of noodles and slurped them up.

"The bastard is down the hall. He may or may not emerge."

"Can I burst a water pipe over his head?"

"I don't think there *is* a water pipe in the ceiling—and if there were, my sister probably wouldn't approve of bursting it."

Pepper pointed her fork at me. "Good point."

Luella and Raphael joined us at the bar. "Thank you for the food, Pepper," said Luella.

"I was hungry. Figured you guys might be, too."

We helped ourselves to egg rolls, noodles, and bite-sized bits of meat in sauce. Raphael and Luella sat on the couch. I pulled a chair close so we could confer without being overheard.

Pepper took a seat on the carpet and set her plate on the coffee table. "So how are we going to get him to come out?"

"Let's freeze him out," said Luella.

"There's no chance of making him like one of those explorers they found frozen solid in Antarctica, is there?" asked Pepper.

Raphael rubbed his chin. "Would that be a bad thing?"

"No, but it would be a little hard to explain," I said.

"I think we can freeze him out without actually turning him into a popsicle," said Luella. She set down her plate.

"Here's what we'll do. I'll push the air into his room. Rose, you pull the heat out of it. Keep the cold air blowing until he comes out."

"And if he goes to the bathroom," said Pepper, "he's mine."

Raphael made a face.

"Raphael, you have any ideas?" I asked.

"If you need someone to throw dirt around, I'm your guy."

"Fair enough. Luella, you ready?"

"Ready." The air sparkled with silver as Luella set her magic into motion.

I kept half of my focus on Damon's heat signature while tracking the movement of Luella's magic.

The cloud of air magic wafted down the hallway. The air currents felt different than water—less concentrated, more diffused—like trying to catch a million microscopic silver butterflies in a net made of magic. I drew away the heat, and Luella pushed the drafts into his room.

Pepper and Raphael watched us with anticipation.

Five minutes of icy wind later, Damon emerged. When he didn't go in the bathroom, Pepper visibly slumped with disappointment. He collected a heavy duty outdoor yoga mat from the hall closet and shoved earbuds in his ears, not deigning to greet anyone as he walked through the living room.

The back door banged open and shut.

We looked at each other, then raced to the window where we could watch through the gaps in the blinds.

"Well, we managed to chase him outside," I said. "Now what?"

Damon rolled out the mat, unaware that we were watching. When Izzy did yoga, the motion was serene, even beautiful—but when Damon did the same poses, he managed to communicate arrogance with his body language alone.

I turned away from the window. "A stack of brochures and a few malfunctioning appliances aren't enough. We need something bigger." My hands balled into fists as I paced.

"Stop before you wear a hole in your sister's carpet," said Luella.

I stopped pacing. "It won't be her carpet for long, not if Damon has anything to do with it."

Raphael spoke without turning his gaze from the backyard. "Ladies, I think you ought to see this."

I returned to the window. Zephyr, Luella's white-and-silver magical dog, crossed the backyard with Horatio a few steps behind her. The two magical familiars sat on their haunches, facing Damon, with the air of an audience waiting for something interesting to happen.

"What are they doing?" Pepper risked pulling one of the slats a little higher for a better look.

"They're watching him," I said. "You think they know something we don't?"

Raphael's forehead creased. "I think I might have an idea."

19

I looked away from the outdoor scene and stared at Raphael. "I refuse to entertain hope until you tell me what it is."

He made a placating gesture. "This is a little ... iffy."

"I don't like iffy."

"What if—stay with me on this—what if he thought the house was about to be swallowed by a sinkhole?"

"A sinkhole?" It came out louder than I intended, and everyone hushed me.

"A sinkhole," said Raphael. "Fastest way to convince someone that their house is about to become a literal money pit. Believe me, I should know."

"How can you do that without cracking my sister's house in half?"

"If I make it localized, it won't affect the house."

I looked outside. Damon was about thirty feet away from the house. "You're sure you won't bring the house down like a pile of Lincoln Logs?"

"Ninety-nine percent sure." He paused. "Maybe ninety-five."

My hand went to the orange gem I'd been wearing since Mrs. Millefleur gave it to me. I rubbed the smooth cabochon with my thumb. Words from my favorite play came to me as if written in letters of fire: *Our doubts are traitors, and make us lose the good we oft might win, by fearing to attempt.* "Do it," I said.

Raphael brought his hands up. He pushed them apart in slow motion like Moses commanding the Red Sea.

Luella, Pepper, and I watched as silver mist trickled out of the ground under Damon's yoga mat.

I spared a brief thought for my sister's xeriscaping. It would be worth the damage—if this worked.

Strain appeared on Raphael's face. The silver mist increased as if pouring from a magic smoke machine.

The gem that rested on my chest glowed faintly. I touched it; it was warm like a stone left in full sun.

The ground rumbled. Volleys of dirt shot into the air, and the earth collapsed under Damon's feet. He tumbled into the hole without even time to shout.

My jaw dropped. "Nice job, Raphael." The ground next to the house was untouched.

Raphael grinned and wiped the sweat from his brow. Then he took a bow. "Thank you. I'll be here all week."

Luella kissed Raphael soundly.

Meanwhile, Damon crawled out of the hole. He rolled onto the grass and stared up at the sky, his chest heaving.

Horatio and Zephyr observed from the sidelines—then a rustle in the bushes caught their attention.

A pointed brown face with twitching silver whiskers peeked out of the bougainvillea hedge.

"It's a raccoon!" cried Pepper.

The raccoon emerged from the hedge and bumbled amiably over to Horatio and Zephyr. The animals touched noses and exchanged polite sniffs.

Raphael pressed his face close to the window glass, no longer seeming to care whether Damon saw him or not. "Look at that adorable little trash panda."

My gaze shifted from the trio of animals to Damon. "He doesn't see it, does he? The raccoon?"

Joy dawned on Raphael's face. "If he doesn't see the raccoon …"

Luella lit up. "Then it's yours?"

They seized each other's hands in a mutual expression of pure happiness.

I had to stop them from rushing outside. "Cool your jets. If you run out there and start cuddling what appears to be thin air …"

"Right. Stay calm," Raphael said to himself. "How about this? We go outside to investigate the noise we heard—then I grab my trash panda and we make a run for it."

Pepper continued to look out the window. "He's getting up."

Damon got to his feet and attempted to brush off the dirt that coated him from head to toe.

"What's the raccoon doing?" said Luella.

The raccoon sidled up to Damon and looked him up and down. After sizing him up, the raccoon pressed its paw on the ground next to Damon's foot.

A mini-earthquake rattled the glass in the window. Another hole opened up, this one smaller—and directly under Damon's foot. His foot dropped into the hole, and the rest of him fell sideways into the bougainvillea hedge.

I winced. Bougainvillea thorns were long as nails and twice as sharp.

"Looks like the raccoon doesn't like him, either," said Luella.

The three animals ran off, paws a-flying.

Damon crawled out of the hedge and got to his feet again. He left the yoga mat in the hole and headed for the back door of the house.

We abandoned the window and ran for the living room just in time for him to walk in.

"And *that's* how I got my kids to eat their vegetables," said Pepper, improvising none too convincingly.

"Great job," said Luella.

"Brilliant," I added. I couldn't help watching Damon out of the corner of my eye. The sight of his filthy clothes was a joy topped only by the array of angry-looking scratches on his arms.

He picked up a condo brochure I'd left out on the bar.

My stomach seized in a spasm of delight. Had the sinkhole pushed him to the edge?

He appeared to reconsider whatever he'd come inside for; instead, he stuffed the brochure in his back pocket, turned on his heel, and went straight back outside without saying a word.

Luella, Pepper, Raphael and I traded confused expressions.

Pepper leaned in. "Why didn't he mention the, you know, *giant sinkhole* that opened up under his feet?"

"I don't know, but I'm going to see what he's doing now." I jumped up and returned to the window.

Damon retrieved a shovel from the shed. He pulled the yoga mat out of the hole and tossed it to the side.

"What's he doing?" said Raphael.

"He's filling in the hole."

"What? Why?" said Luella.

The three of them rushed to join me at the window.

"Don't let him see you," I said.

We watched through the cracks in the blinds as Damon filled in first the larger hole, then the smaller one, as fast as he could shovel.

"Why would he cover it up?" asked Pepper.

"He's hiding it." My mind raced. If I were Damon, why would I hide the sinkhole?

When he was done, he carefully smoothed the ground and put away the shovel.

Luella, Pepper, Raphael, and I retreated, lest we be caught when he came in.

Damon entered the house with a satisfied look on his face—an odd expression to have when you're covered in dirt and scratches after falling into a hole.

It would be suspiciously out of character for me to show any interest in his activities at all—but if I wanted to know what that smug expression was about, I had a choice between talking to him, or reading his mind. I didn't relish the thought of having my magic anywhere near his nasty little conniving brain. "Did you have a nice ... yoga?"

He looked at me like I'd lost my mind. "Since when are you interested in what I do?"

"Just trying to be civil," I said.

He grunted and turned away to rummage in the fridge.

The exchange had clarified precisely nothing. To hell with any dainty ethical reservations—Mrs. Millefleur was right.

This was war.

I steeled myself, pushed out with my magic, and brushed against his thoughts. I captured only one impression before my disgust became so strong it broke the connection: *If the house needs fixing, she can pay for it.* I shuddered.

Damon disappeared down the hallway.

Everyone was staring at me.

"You okay, Rose? You look sick," said Pepper.

"Yes. No. I ... I read Damon's thoughts."

They leaned back apprehensively, as if they might be next.

"It's not like that! I'm not reading your minds. Calm down."

"Did it work, then?" asked Luella.

"Oh, it worked. But it was like licking shower mold." I paused. "He's happy. He thinks the sinkhole will bankrupt Izzy."

Pepper let out a stream of creative swearing that encompassed Damon's parentage, shortcomings, and afterlife status.

I raised my hands to stop the flood. "If he thinks that, so much the better. He'll walk away from the house thinking he got the best of the bargain."

Pepper muttered something about alligators.

"Speaking of animals," said Luella, "how about that raccoon?"

Raphael straightened. "My trash panda! How do I get it to come back?"

I stood and shook off the lingering distaste of touching Damon's thoughts. "Follow me. I have an idea."

We put on our jackets, and Luella and Raphael put on their matching hats. I leashed Braveheart, who always appreciated a little exercise, and led the way to the forest at the edge of the neighborhood. We trekked over the pine needles until we reached a clearing.

"Horatio!" I called.

"Zephyr!" said Luella.

Pepper and Raphael looked around expectantly.

The magical animals emerged from the underbrush: first Zephyr, then the raccoon, then Horatio bringing up the rear.

Braveheart let out a happy bark.

Raphael crouched and held his hands out to the raccoon. "Come here, you little trash panda. Come to Papa."

The raccoon walked to Raphael. It sat on its haunches and raised its forepaws to Raphael's face, patting his cheeks and tugging his short beard. Its paws left behind twinkles of magic that sparkled briefly in the sun, like frost, before disappearing.

Luella spoke in a hushed voice. "What are you going to call her?"

Raphael scooped up the raccoon and held it in his arms. "Princess." He nuzzled her head and looked absolutely smitten.

Luella, Pepper, and I snickered.

"What? Can't a man love a raccoon?" He smoothed her flank. "Don't listen to them, Princess. They're just jealous."

I lifted Horatio and held him tight. His radiant warmth heated my cheek as I rested it against his head.

Maybe—just maybe—everything would turn out all right.

20

The white circus tent towered over the fairgrounds. A "Circus Aetherium" banner flapped in slow motion over the entrance, its text rimmed with gold and surrounded by silver flourishes. The winter breeze carried the scent of popcorn into the night.

Our group huddled together against the cold. Raphael and Luella sported their matching hats. Luella's mother was almost unrecognizable in a thick, quilted coat that went all the way to her knees. "Dang this cold weather," she said.

Izzy tugged on the girls' jackets, making sure their hoods were up and the zippers pulled all the way to the top.

Astrid rolled her eyes. "Mom, it's Florida, not the frozen tundra."

Pepper and her family held an assortment of snacks from the nearby food cart. Her boys, Rocky and Kevin, practically vibrated with excitement.

Kevin hopped from foot to foot. "Do they have lions, Mom? Huh? Do they?"

Pepper's husband, Pete, adjusted his thick-framed glasses and surveyed the scene as the crowd gathered in front of the entrance. "Hmm … I expect we will find out," he said. "Looks like they're letting people in."

I pulled my black leather jacket tighter and followed them through the tent opening.

A woman in a red majorette costume collected our tickets in a rectangular vending tray. When I handed over my ticket, she winked. "Enjoy the show."

We made our way to the risers that surrounded the circus ring on three sides. The tent was smaller and more intimate than it appeared from the outside, and it warmed quickly from the spectators' body heat. Pete led the way into an empty riser, followed by the boys and Pepper, then Raphael, Luella, Mama, and Izzy and the girls. I settled at the end of the riser.

Despite Mama being several seats away, her voice suddenly filled my ears as if I were wearing headphones. *Remember to not freak out, Rose—you hear me?*

I'd forgotten her air magic included telepathy. I leaned forward to make eye contact with her down the row. When I did, I raised a skeptical eyebrow.

Mama gave me a saucy grin in return. Whatever the surprise was, she wasn't telling.

Dreamlike circus music drifted from the speakers. The sound felt lulling until it struck the occasional discordant note.

Sadie stood and waved her arms in an improvised interpretive dance while the adults looked on and smiled.

When the risers were full, the lights dimmed.

The crowd fell silent under the spell of the dim golden lights and the meandering circus melody.

The ticket-taker—now the ringmaster—stepped into the center spotlight. Her voice carried clearly without a visible microphone. "Welcome, one and all, to the Circus Aetherium! Tonight we present wonders beyond imagination and spectacles that defy explanation. We invite you to sit back, relax... and join us on a journey of fire, air, water, and earth." With a flourish of her cane, she retreated to the rear of the ring and disappeared in darkness.

When the lights revived, a woman appeared in the ring. Shiny coins on her midnight-colored costume glinted as she moved with snakelike grace through a series of body-bending movements. Her exposed belly fluttered and rolled in time with the music. Tiny ornaments on her torso and arms twinkled in the light.

The dancer lifted an oval ring with spikes from the floor. She raised it over her head, showcasing the shape—like an elongated sun with short rays—and brought it down over her body to settle on her hips. With a flourish and a snap of her fingers, silver sparks ignited balls of real fire at the tip of each ray.

I gasped. That was no circus trick, no magic sleight-of-hand. That was *fire magic*.

Down the row, Pepper clapped her hands over her mouth. Luella and her mother cheered, and Raphael just sat with his mouth hanging open.

Thankfully, the rest of the crowd was also impressed—for slightly different reasons—and our reactions did not stand out.

Mama's voice arrived in my ears again. *Not freaking out, are you?*

I wished I had telepathy, too, so I could talk back. I had a million questions. Instead, I focused my attention on the dancer.

The little fireballs shook back and forth as she kept a swishing rhythm with her hips. In a dramatic pause, all of the fireballs went out. When the next beat sounded, the ends of the spokes flared a magical silver and reignited in perfect time with the music.

I couldn't believe I was watching another fire witch at work. It was all I could do to stay in my seat, when I would have preferred to drag the dancer away, buy her a cup of coffee, and talk shop for hours.

Also, to get some wardrobe tips.

She finished her routine with a dizzying spin that ended with a dramatic drop to the floor as the flames—and the spotlight—extinguished, leaving the tent in near-complete darkness.

The musical theme changed, and the lights came up on a pair of women dressed in green satin bullfighter costumes. They wore their hair pulled tight in sleek and shiny topknots. Each brandished a fistful of knives to the audience.

They spaced themselves across the ring. Each juggler tossed the knives into a flashing spin. They pivoted to face each other, and the blades flashed across the space between them. The knives flew higher and faster, weaving unnatural paths between the two jugglers, paths that would have been impossible without some sort of trick. From the slipstream of silver that flowed between them, it appeared the jugglers were controlling the flight of the knives with air magic.

The audience remained silent in rapt attention as the jugglers directed the knives upward in a startling series of throws. The knives hung in the air for a beat longer than would have been possible, then fell like missiles, thunking into the ground point first in rapid succession.

The audience clapped and cheered.

Mama and Luella added their own whoops and hollers like they were rooting for their home team.

Pepper, Raphael, and I shared looks of wonder before our attention returned to the floor.

The green-clad juggler witches took a deep bow, retrieved their knives, and ran offstage.

The lights shifted up, illuminating a swath of purple silk that tumbled from the highest point of the tent. A woman in a matching purple unitard struck a pose beneath the cloth, then hooked the cloth around her ankle and used it to pull herself upward. Near the top of the silk, she used an intricate series of movements to wrap herself into the fabric.

After a pose, she released her grip. The twists unraveled, allowing her to tumble downward in a controlled fall until she stopped halfway down the silk.

From there, she lifted her body—with what must have been near-superhuman strength—parallel to the silk.

Billows of silver mist appeared. Wind pushed the aerialist around and around in a tight spin. When the magic dissipated, the spin stopped. Once more the aerialist climbed.

From an upside down position high above the circus floor, with her uppermost leg already wrapped in silk, she looped the fabric over the other leg and allowed a long loop of slack to dangle.

Astrid leaned forward in anticipation. "She's going to do a big drop."

I couldn't help leaning forward, too.

Instead of the anticipated drop, the aerialist spasmed—not like a performer preparing her next move, but like a person racked with pain.

Something was wrong.

The other circus performers, who must have been just outside the ring of light, came running from every direction—only to drop like felled trees. They lay motionless in the dirt.

Then, the aerialist's head lolled. Her grip slackened.

The audience gasped.

I reached with both hands as if I could stop what was happening by sheer will—but before any of us could do anything, the aerialist fell.

With the sound of a hundred cannon, the dirt floor of the circus exploded as if it had been punched from below. The geyser of earth seemed to envelop the aerialist mid-fall, obscuring her descent to the ground.

When the dust cleared, she lay limp on the ground under the swinging silk.

The fire dancer woke from whatever had struck her down. She sat up and held her hands out with an expression of dismay. Then she scrambled to the fallen aerialist's side.

Was she breathing? Had the explosion somehow cushioned the fall?

The other performers ran to help. With a small crowd around the aerialist, she could no longer be seen.

I was holding my breath when the knot of people finally parted. Thank all the stars—the aerialist was alive and unbroken. The jugglers helped her to her feet. She managed a shaky wave, and the entire line of performers took a bow.

The scent of smoke distracted me from the scene unfolding in the ring. I sniffed, then looked down at my chest and realized the fire opal had gotten so hot it was scorching my shirt. I hastily unclasped it and held it by the chain.

The last time the gem got warm, Raphael had blown a hole in Izzy's backyard. Did it heat up in the presence of earth magic? No one but an earth witch—and a very powerful one, at that—could have caught someone in midair with a volley of dirt. I snapped my fingers at Raphael to get his attention. "Was that you?" I said.

He shook his head emphatically.

The fire dancer stepped forward. "Ladies and gentlemen, we are experiencing some technical difficulties and will be unable to finish our show tonight."

Grumbles and a few scattered boos swept through the crowd.

"But," she continued, "we will be glad to honor your tickets at a future show."

Behind her, the other performers exchanged apprehensive looks.

While the disappointed crowd prepared to depart, I closed my eyes and pushed my awareness outward, away from the heat of the crowd, outside the tent and into the cold night. The food cart glowed with the heat of its cooking appliances. I kept searching.

There—near the edge of the fairground—a lone heat signature moved in the direction of the forest.

I opened my eyes, then stood and tucked the cooled necklace into my pocket. "Excuse me," I said as I squeezed past Izzy and the girls to get further down the row. I leaned down to Luella, Mama, Raphael, and Pepper, and spoke quietly so I couldn't be overheard. "Someone out there is running away. We need to get outside before this crowd does."

Pepper made as if to leap to her feet.

"Not you," I said. "You take your family and get clear of here until we know what's going on."

"Aw, man," said Pepper. "I never get to have any fun."

Luella stood. "I'm coming."

Raphael followed her lead.

"I'll go talk to the performers," said Mama. "This was supposed to be a fun surprise, not a"—she gestured in the direction of the ring—"whatever the hell that was."

"Fine. Luella, Raphael, let's go." I turned around to find Izzy staring at me.

"Rose?"

I pressed my lips together, caught between the need to get out before I lost the trail, and the need to reassure my sister. "I'll explain everything. Just—not right now. I'll see you back at your house. Promise." It would have to do.

I pushed past with Luella and Raphael behind me.

We ducked under a loose tent flap and ran into the night.

21

We made it to the edge of the fairground before all three of us had to stop. The cold air burned my lungs as I tried to catch my breath.

"How much," said Raphael between gasps, "further?"

I pressed my hands to my forehead. "If whoever it is gets in a car on the other side of that scrub, we've lost them."

Luella spread her arms. Her wings unfolded like tracings of moonlight. "We haven't lost them yet."

"You can't go after some unknown witch alone," said Raphael.

Luella smiled. "Why not? Wouldn't be the first time."

"No, Raphael's right. It could be dangerous." My hands balled into fists and I pushed them over my hair in an attempt to think straight. "Horatio!"

The cat appeared at my feet.

"Horatio can track people, I think. He did it with Mrs. Millefleur downtown." I knelt next to him and stroked his head. "If you follow him, you can cut the runner off from the road. Keep your distance, though."

"Right," said Luella. "We certainly don't want them to see a flying woman."

"Exactly. Knock them down with air, if you must. We'll close the gap from this side. If we hurry, we can catch them between us."

Luella nodded. "Got it. Zephyr!" The dog appeared in a flurry of leaves. "You ready to play fetch, girl?" Luella lifted her wings and hovered in place.

Horatio bounded into the undergrowth, followed by Zephyr.

Luella flew after them.

Raphael and I entered the scrub. It was hard to see in the dark, and we tripped over exposed roots in our haste, but we kept going without a light. We didn't want our quarry to see us coming.

Luella's voice arrived in my ears as Mama's had earlier. *I see someone through the trees. He's almost at the road. I'm circling around and going low. Zephyr will crash through the underbrush and make enough noise to scare him back toward you.*

"He?" said Raphael, who had obviously heard the same message.

A crashing sound carried through the forest.

I ignited silver fire in both hands, in case I needed to flame something. "Be ready if he tries to dodge."

We broke through a thicket and into a small clearing. The forest continued on the other side of the clearing, about twenty feet away.

A figure burst out of the underbrush across from us.

I held up my hand. "Stop!"

The figure skidded to a halt.

"Don't move."

The man took one impertinent step out of the shadows. The moonlight revealed a handsome face—and the familiar lines of a well-cut black overcoat. "Dear Rose! Fancy meeting you here."

I froze.

"Do you know this guy?" said Raphael.

I nodded, not trusting myself to speak. Not only did I know him, but I'd kissed him.

Twice.

Luella emerged from the woods behind Oliver. Horatio and Zephyr moved into flanking positions on either side of him.

I stared at Oliver. "You want to explain what you were doing at the circus?"

"Oh, I adore a good circus."

"So you decided to run into the wilderness afterward?"

"Lovely night for a stroll." He glanced over his shoulder, acknowledging Luella's presence. "Astonishingly, you and your friends thought so as well."

"Rose, who is this?" said Luella.

"Mrs. Millefleur's chauffeur. Oliver."

"This is *Oliver*? The Oliver you—"

"Yes," I said. My mind worked furiously. Something had gone terribly wrong at the circus. Something most likely magical. But it also appeared that magic—*earth* magic—had saved the aerialist from certain death.

A near-tragedy, and a miracle. Bad magic, good magic.

And someone—no, not just someone, *Oliver*—fled into the night immediately after.

My heartbeat slowed. Logic flowed through my veins like ice water. Was Oliver a *witch*? If he was a witch, was he the rescuer—or the perpetrator? His countenance, as smooth as ever, gave no hint. Except…he appeared to be waiting for me to put the pieces together, waiting for me to come to some sort of conclusion.

Pieces clicked into place, one after the other, like clockwork that couldn't be stopped.

"He's a witch," I said.

Luella gasped.

Oliver's eyes narrowed slightly, and a half-smile lifted the corner of his lips.

Raphael looked back and forth between Oliver and me. "Does that mean he attacked the aerialist, or he saved her?"

I hadn't broken eye contact with Oliver. "Well?"

"Would you believe me if I told you?"

"I might."

He laughed. "Why don't you just try what you did at the Christmas market? Or the club?"

My cheeks burned.

"You're not squeamish about it now, are you?"

I charged across the clearing and grabbed him by the lapels of his overcoat. "Push me, Oliver, and I will crisp you where you stand."

He stood still in my grasp, seemingly unaffected—or, worse, *enjoying* himself. "Crisp me if you will, Rose, but the real culprit escapes your grasp. Someone fled the circus before me. I was tracking them when they vanished."

"It was you who saved the aerialist."

"'Save' is such a strong word."

I restrained the urge to light him up like a s'more. "How about 'stopped her from falling to her death'? Does that satisfy you?"

"Immensely, coming from you."

I met Luella's gaze over Oliver's shoulder. "Luella? What do you think?"

"Your call," she said.

I regarded Oliver. I had no concrete reason to trust him. Though a small, treacherous portion of my soul danced in glee to know that Oliver was a witch, the rest of it seethed that he'd been lying to me all along. Then again, I hadn't exactly been open with the fact that I was a witch, either. Neither of us had trusted the other with the truth.

But Luella and Pepper were right. I couldn't go full Millefleur.

I let go of his lapels. "I won't try to read your mind." I expected him to sigh with relief.

He did not.

Instead, he took my hand and gently kissed it. "That is one of the things I like most about you. You are, at heart, a deeply moral person."

"I am not." My skin was still tingling from the kiss. "I tried to read your mind before. Twice," I added.

"If you were not deeply moral, those attempts would not have troubled you," he said.

Horatio's paws crackled the leaves on the floor of the clearing. He sat by my foot and rubbed his face against my leg. His soothing purr calmed me. "I know I can trust you,"

I said to Oliver, "because you know that if you're lying, I will turn you into a pile of ash."

He responded with tenderness, as if I had not just threatened his life. "Because you have trusted me, I will trust you in return." He kissed my forehead. "Read my mind."

"You *want* me to—"

"I trust that you will not go rummaging around in there. Time is of the essence, fire witch. The sooner you confirm that I am who and what I say I am, the sooner we can find the true villain."

"Are you sure?"

"I'm sure."

I brushed the contours of his consciousness. Beneath the veil of my magic, the map of his mind sparkled.

I touched the foremost point of light with great delicacy.

His expression remained calm but for a slight flinch.

The memory revealed the circus through his eyes. Fear surged through me when the aerialist fell. Oliver's earth magic thundered through me as if it were my own. The sheer force of it made me stumble against him. He held me in his arms as the rest of the memory played out: the flight into the forest to find the perpetrator, and finally his memory of facing me across the clearing. How much admiration he had felt for me—and so much fear that I would reject him.

My chest hurt. I withdrew from the connection with his mind, and buried my face in the space between his neck and shoulder. "Oliver—I didn't know …"

"Hush, dear Rose." He held me tight.

"I'm sorry I said I would turn you into a pile of ash."

"Anyone who betrayed you would deserve it."

"This is fantastic," said Raphael, with undisguised enthusiasm. "If you're the one who threw all that dirt around ... then you're like me—you're an earth witch! You can teach me!"

I raised my head and shot him a stony look for interrupting the moment.

Oliver spared Raphael a glance that took in his knitted ski hat. "Let joy be unconfined."

Luella crossed the clearing in a businesslike manner, followed by Zephyr. "Now that we're all sorted out, and seeing as how whoever did this isn't currently hanging around in the woods, perhaps we should head back and see what's going on?"

I cleared my throat and slid out of Oliver's warm embrace. Somehow, I'd gotten a little distracted. "Definitely."

We followed Luella and Raphael out of the woods. When we reached the open ground surrounding the circus tent, Mama's crow, Midnight—or just "Crow," if you asked Mama—swooped across the empty space and landed on the roof of the food cart. He fixed us with a black pearl of a stare.

Mama emerged from the circus tent. "You all coming?" she said. "We got a problem."

22

Without a crowd to fill it up, the circus tent took on a melancholy appearance. Mama led the way to an empty riser down front.

Luella looked around. "Where are all the circus performers?"

"After what they went through, I sent them off to rest. This is our territory and our responsibility to fix." Mama caught sight of Oliver and held up a hand. "Hang on a second. We can't talk freely around no strangers." She peered at him more closely. "Wait a minute—you're Hilda's driver."

Oliver acknowledged the statement with a polite nod. "And you are?"

"In charge." She kept her eyes on Oliver. "Rose, did you bring this one along?"

"We tracked him down outside. He's a witch."

"Oh, is he now?" Mama threw her hands up. "This whole damn town is suddenly crawling with witches."

"I assure you—"

"Quiet, sonny. I don't know you—and I don't trust you, neither. Why's Hilda got a witch driving her car?"

"I am her bodyguard."

Mama's eyes widened. "You ain't serious."

"Deadly serious."

Mama paced in front of the empty stands. Her long, thick coat made her look like an agitated penguin. "I don't suppose you'd care to tell me what's going on?"

"That would be my employer's prerogative, unfortunately."

"Damn that woman and her secrets." Mama rounded on Oliver. "If you're her bodyguard, why are you here? Why aren't you guarding her?"

"She sent me here."

"Why?"

"She was concerned something would happen tonight."

"You caught the high-flyer, didn't you?"

"I did."

"Huh." Mama's gaze sharpened into an appraisal. "Pretty powerful, then, aren't you?"

"Yes." No banter, no false modesty.

"Interesting," Mama mused. "What do you say we pay Hilda a visit?"

"I'd say she wouldn't like that at all," said Oliver.

"Good. About time she starts suffering the consequences of keeping secrets from her fellow witches. Rose, you know how to get to Hilda's house?"

"No …"

"Old tea-and-crumpets here can tell you. Isn't that right?" Mama slapped Oliver on the back.

"It's Oliver, madam."

But Mama was already on the move, and didn't respond. She hooked her arms through Luella's and Raphael's and practically dragged them away.

Oliver watched the trio march out of the tent. "How did we have an entire conversation with that remarkable woman, and yet I know absolutely nothing more than when I first walked in?"

"Welcome to my world." I stood. "Well, we won't get any more answers just standing around." I crooked my elbow and held it out.

He eyed the arm I offered. "Are you sure you won't crisp me?"

"Not unless you change the music in my truck. Come on, I'll drop you off at your car." We walked outside. I unlocked the truck and climbed into the driver's seat.

Oliver's chauffeur habits must have kicked in, for he held the door for me until I was seated, then closed it before entering on the passenger side.

The circus tent receded in the rearview mirror. I followed the road around the trees bordering the fairgrounds, then pulled onto the shoulder behind where Oliver had discreetly parked Mrs. Millefleur's white Town Car.

After he gave me directions to her house, Oliver got out and cast me one more look through the open door.

Our eyes met. Whatever was between us crossed the space like an electrical arc.

"See you there," I said.

"Goodbye, Rose." He shut the door and walked away.

The truck tires spun on the loose gravel as I hit the gas. I had no need to follow Oliver—I knew Sparkle Beach like the back of my hand. I summoned Horatio, who settled in his usual shotgun spot.

Thanks to the late hour, traffic was sparse between the fairgrounds and the beachside. Mrs. Millefleur's beachfront house lay behind a black metal gate tipped with gold spikes. The gates were open, and Luella's car was already parked in the circular drive.

I parked, then patted my shoulder. Horatio obligingly leaped to ride along.

The house rose above us. Flat coquina stones covered the exterior, and a Roman arch framed the double front door.

The wrought iron handle was in my grasp when my phone buzzed in my back pocket.

Pepper's text appeared in our group chat. *Will someone please tell me what is going on?*

My fingers flew. *More than I can share in a text, that's for sure.*

Pepper sent back a semi-nonsensical stream of emojis that seemed to indicate frustration—at least, that's what I assumed from the explosion, the fireball, and the cat face emoji that appeared to be screaming.

I pulled open the front door and entered.

An oyster shell chandelier hung over the soaring entry-way. I passed underneath it and found Luella and Raphael sitting in a spacious sunken living room. Luella had summoned Zephyr, who sat at alert as Luella nervously ran her hand over the dog's back. Mama's jacket lay over the back of the couch, and Mama paced in front of the wide bank of picture windows facing the ocean.

She stopped. "Hilda, nobody cares about the damn tea!"

Mrs. Millefleur bustled into the room with a tray of tea things and set it on the coffee table.

The front door opened and shut. Oliver entered the room, shrugged off his overcoat, and laid it next to Mama's puffy jacket monstrosity.

Mrs. Millefleur addressed him without looking up from pouring the tea. "Was it as I predicted, Oliver?"

"Quite." He took a cup.

Raphael eyed the tea tray. "None for me, thanks."

Mrs. Millefleur raised an imperious eyebrow. "If I wanted to kill you, I would have done so already."

"You nearly did," he replied.

"Nonsense." Mrs. Millefleur sipped her tea.

"Everybody settle down," said Mama. "We ain't got time for bickering."

It had been a long night. I took a teacup and balanced a pair of cookies on its saucer.

Luella did the same.

Raphael abstained.

After a show of looking around to see if anyone else would break the silence, Mama continued. "Somebody tried to do something to the circus witches' powers."

Oliver and Mrs. Millefleur briefly locked eyes, then looked back at Mama.

"If old tea-and-crumpets hadn't been there, it could have been a lot uglier," she continued. "How did you know to send him, Hilda?"

Mrs. Millefleur shifted. "I heard rumors."

Mama put her hands on her hips. "Don't piss on my leg and tell me it's raining."

Mrs. Millefleur's eyes widened and she drew herself up. "I am not—"

"Now see here, Hilda Millefleur. I've let you get away with too much for too long. Just 'cause you're the richest witch in Sparkle Beach doesn't mean you're in charge, and it sure don't mean you're the most powerful. This is my town as much as it is yours, you can bet on that."

Mrs. Millefleur stared into her own tea cup like she was trying to read invisible tea leaves. "If I tell you, it will place you in greater danger."

Mama rounded on Oliver. "What about you, tea-and-crumpets? You gonna share with the class?"

Oliver glanced at Mrs. Millefleur, then met Mama's gaze, saying nothing.

Raphael made a disbelieving noise. "How are we supposed to trust either of you? She threw me off a lighthouse, and you're some sort of secret earth witch bodyguard who's working with her?" He blinked with a sudden realization. "You were there that night. At the lighthouse!"

"After the fact," Oliver replied.

"He wasn't involved," added Mrs. Millefleur.

"So you want the rest of us to sit this out while you handle whatever's going on?" I scoffed. "Not likely."

Mrs. Millefleur's voice rang out. "I can handle it!"

We all looked on in shock. I'd never heard her raise her voice before.

"I should have handled this in the first place," she said, more quietly. "It's my fault. I will fix it. I just wanted all of you to be ... prepared, in case anything happens."

Mama rolled her eyes. "But something *did* happen. And if we don't know what *else* could happen, Hilda, how the hell can we be prepared?"

Mrs. Millefleur squeezed her eyes shut, then reopened them with an expression of resolve. She set down her tea and moved to sit next to me on the couch. "I shouldn't have chastised you about your ... *interaction* with Oliver. I was afraid of what you might learn from him. I apologize."

My skin prickled. Mrs. Millefleur, apologizing? What was happening? Something was deeply off-base.

She took my hand and patted it. "I'm sorry."

My instincts screamed a warning. I tried to pull back my hand. "What are you—"

Time seemed to stop. I couldn't pull away. All ambient sound disappeared like the room had been put on mute.

In that silent, everlasting moment, new magic coursed from her fingers to mine. It rolled through my arm and slammed into my body in shock waves. The incoming power felt as if it might blast my soul right out of my body.

I opened my mouth in a wordless cry, but nothing came out. I was dying—I was being reborn—surrounded by yet separate from my friends, all of us locked in a frozen tableau.

Oliver's tea cup floated in midair, and I became aware, vaguely, that he had dropped it in his rush to get to me. Now he hung, arrested in mid-motion, halfway to his intended destination.

Fire sizzled through my veins starting at the tips of my toes and burning its way upward until it seized my head like a flaming vise. I cried out again, and this time the sound emerged as if from a record suddenly sped up to full speed.

The floating cup crashed to the floor. Oliver's arms went around me. "What have you done?" he said.

I knew, though he did not specify, that he was speaking to Mrs. Millefleur. Stray thoughts from every person in the room beat against my mind like birds against a window. I pressed my hands to my ears. "Stop it—I can't think!" I turned to Mrs. Millefleur. "What did you do to me?"

"I gave you the rest of my magic."

"What? Why?" Even the sound of my own voice hurt.

My friends' anger and confusion on my behalf only increased the cacophony in my head. Horatio let out a howl of unhappiness. I cuddled him to my chest and rocked back and forth. "Make it stop."

"Pardon me," said Oliver. His fingers delved into my pocket and came up with the fire opal necklace I'd removed earlier. He held the stone in a tight grip, then placed the chain around my neck.

Instantly, the ringing, intrusive thoughts quieted. "What did you do?" I asked.

"A small defensive spell. You are very sensitive right now."

He was warm, and I was tired. I rested against him. "I feel sick …"

"Hush, now. It will pass." He shot Mrs. Millefleur a castigating look. "You shouldn't have pushed so much magic on her so quickly."

Mrs. Millefleur stood. "As you said, the discomfort will pass. It is better for me to give up my powers. It is better for her to be as powerful as she can be." Her gaze shifted pointedly to Luella. "Perhaps someday you will understand. And now, I shall retire. Oliver, you must take her home. She is in no fit state to drive." With that, Mrs. Millefleur ascended the staircase, her steps deliberate and heavy, as if she carried a great weight. She turned back halfway and looked at Oliver. "Go ahead and tell them," she said. She continued up the stairs without another word and disappeared into the second floor.

All eyes turned to Oliver.

"Tell us what?" said Mama.

Oliver sighed. "There is … a witch who is not a witch. A thief of magic. Mrs. Millefleur had a—I suppose you could call it a 'truce'—with her. Perhaps 'non-interference pact' is a better phrase."

"And?" said Mama.

"What happened at the circus indicates that the truce is over. The thief breached Mrs. Millefleur's territory. All bets are off."

Luella looked confused. "But why would Mrs. Millefleur make a truce in the first place?"

Oliver paused and smoothed a few strands of hair away from my face. "Because the magic thief is Mrs. Millefleur's sister."

23

Raphael and Oliver helped me into the Town Car. Mrs. Millefleur was right about one thing—I was in no state to drive. I curled against the plush leather seat and watched the streetlights pass in blurry streaks. I hadn't felt so out of it since my wisdom teeth were removed under anaesthesia when I was in high school.

When the car stopped, it took me a moment to register that we were at my cabin rather than Izzy's house. I sat up, which was a mistake, as the movement made the world spin around in circles. "No ... I have to go to Izzy's—"

"Nonsense," said Oliver, with crisp authority. "Your idiot brother-in-law can wait. You must rest." He exited the vehicle and opened the door on my side.

I leaned out far enough to see Luella, Mama, and Raphael standing by. They'd brought my truck.

I fell bonelessly against the seat and closed my eyes. "Tell Oliver I need to go to Izzy's."

"Old tea-and-crumpets is right," said Mama. "You need a good night's sleep."

Luella leaned down. "I'll stay with you and make sure you're all right."

Under the weight of their concern, I could do nothing but concede. They bundled me into the house. The air had that unlived-in smell houses get when unoccupied for more than a day or two. "Can someone please text Izzy and let her know?" I didn't trust my fumbly fingers.

Luella and Mama steered me to the couch to recuperate while they disappeared down the hall to turn down my bed. Oliver knelt and removed my shoes like I was some kind of reverse Cinderella.

"You don't have to do that," I said.

He set the boots neatly aside. "If you tried to do it, you'd topple over on your head—and then where would we be?"

Raphael looked around the living room. "No Christmas tree?"

"Haven't had time." A lie was easier than explaining that I only liked other people's Christmas decorations, and strenuously avoided putting up my own.

After helping me into bed, Mama leaned close and tucked the sheets. "Don't you push yourself, now. You're going to need your strength. You hear me?"

I closed my eyes. "I hear you."

Oliver's voice drifted from the doorway. "Does she have the necklace?"

"I think so," said Mama.

The sound of his footsteps told me he'd entered the room, and the scent of wood and citrus let me know he had leaned close. "You should keep it on even while sleeping."

"Bossy old tea-and-crumpets," I murmured.

"Rest well, goth queen."

A smile touched my lips even as sleep beckoned me into darkness.

I dreamed of floating—out of Black Bear Ridge, across town, and over the Intracoastal River, down to the coquina-clad house on Sparkle Beach. The doors swung open before my feet touched the ground, and I had to skip to compensate for landing at a much higher speed than I would have walked.

The black surf rolled on silver sand outside the picture windows. The waves were closer than I remembered seeing them before.

There was no one else in sight.

"Mrs. Millefleur?"

No response.

"Hilda?" Surely that would get a rise out of her, even in a dream.

Nothing.

I crossed the room to a credenza positioned along the far wall. Picture frames lined the top of the credenza at precise intervals: several of Mrs. Millefleur and her late husband, presumably—and a black-and-white photo of two young women.

I lifted the frame to examine the black-and-white photo more closely. Without a doubt, it was a young Mrs. Millefleur, and someone who bore a strong resemblance to her.

Sisters …

I didn't know if I'd said the word aloud, or if it scorched the air by some magic of its own. I remembered Izzy's words: *Do you think I could get some magical powers of my own?*

I pushed up my sleeve and revealed the flaming rose tattoo on my bicep. The flames had taken on a life of their own, wavering and flickering across my skin like the real thing.

I seized the exposed flesh and pinched as hard as I could.

I woke to the warm rumble of Horatio curled against my back. I sat up with care, expecting to feel woozy—but other than lingering fatigue from yet another late night, I felt almost normal.

After showering and getting dressed, I emerged to find Luella sitting in front of the fireplace.

"Don't eat," she said.

"And a good morning to you, too."

Luella chuckled. "Pepper's coming. You know what that means."

"Ah, yes. A full complement of Highway to Grill's breakfast menu, am I right?"

"Winner, winner, chicken dinner. Or chicken breakfast."

"Aren't we all supposed to be at work now?"

"That's the other news—Queenie says the three of us are on paid leave until we get this situation sorted out."

Someone pounded on the door.

"That'll be Pepper." I opened the door to find Pepper holding three white paper bags emblazoned with the Highway to Grill logo.

She shoved the bags into my hands and marched into the living room. "What happened to 'Ride-or-Die' Witches, huh? Did it get changed to 'Ride-or-Maybe-Not' while I wasn't looking? 'Ride-or-Just-Go-Home'? Just because I have kids doesn't mean you can shuffle me off to Buffalo right when things get interesting." Pepper crossed her arms.

Luella spoke in a soothing tone. "No one was trying to—"

"Don't patronize me, Luella."

"She's not patronizing you," I said. "And thank you, by the way, for the food."

Pepper's arms came down from where she had folded them tightly across her chest. "You're welcome. But—"

"Listen. We've never had anything like this happen before. We didn't have a plan ready. Next time, we'll have a plan." I dug in one of the bags—the food smelled too good to ignore. "Have you told your husband about any of this yet?"

Pepper took an angry bite out of a hashbrown and said nothing.

"That's a 'no,' then." I unwrapped a chicken biscuit and shot Luella a look.

Luella picked up where I had left off. "If he doesn't know, how will he take it when you run off for what appears to be no reason?"

"I'll *tell* him. Just—not yet." Pepper looked at her hashbrown as if it were at fault for making her sad. "I don't want to miss out on all the fun …"

"Of course not," said Luella.

"Ride-or-Die Witches forever," I added.

Pepper gave a tentative smile. "I'm sorry I freaked out."

"You wouldn't be you if you didn't," I said.

While we finished breakfast, Luella and I recapped what had happened the previous night. When we were done, Pepper gave a long whistle. "So your guy Oliver is not only hot and British, he's a freaking powerful earth witch, too?"

"He's not 'my guy'—"

Pepper rolled her eyes. "Oh, *obviously.*"

"Seriously, that's what you got out of all that?"

She shrugged.

"Nothing about Mrs. Millefleur's sister, or the fact that she dumped her remaining powers on me? Or that someone tried to steal the circus witches' powers?"

"I *got* it," said Pepper, "I was just addressing the most important issue first."

"You're hopeless," I said.

"A hopeless romantic, you mean." She waggled her eyebrows.

"So what are we going to do about all this?" asked Luella.

"Well—" My thought was interrupted by the distant hum of my phone. "Hang on." I turned in circles, like a dog, in search of the direction of the buzz.

Luella plunged her hand into the couch and retrieved the phone from where it had fallen between the cushions.

A text from Izzy blazed across the screen: *Have you seen Damon?*

I made a face. "Ugh, why would I have seen Damon?" I typed a response: *No, why?*

He left, she wrote. *And he hasn't come back.*

Ha! We win! Should I buy one bottle of champagne, or two? I replied. I added a few jaunty champagne bottle emojis and clinking glass emojis for good measure.

Three dots appeared as Izzy typed. Then the completed message arrived: *No one can find him. He didn't show up to work.*

The triumphant, fizzy feeling screeched to a halt like someone pulled the needle off a record.

24

I dialed Izzy immediately. The phone rang and rang before she picked up on what felt like the millionth ring. "Why don't you answer your phone? And what do you mean, no one can find him?"

"I'm at work. I meant exactly what I said—no one has heard from him."

"Maybe he decided to move out."

"Maybe he did. But why would he have left all his stuff behind?"

I stopped pacing in front of the cold fireplace. "Maybe he went on vacation?"

"Without calling in to work? Damon's a lot of things, but he'd rather die than harm his professional reputation. I don't think he'd skip out without notifying someone."

"He is having a midlife crisis, you know."

Izzy sighed. "I know."

"For all we know, he decided to go find himself in the Himalayas."

That got a laugh. "What happened last night, anyway? Are you okay?"

"I'm fine. Nothing a coffee won't cure. In fact, I'm on my way back to your house right now." I silently signaled to Luella and Pepper to see if they would go with me.

They nodded, then gathered their things and rounded up the breakfast trash.

I returned my attention to the phone. "I'm sure Damon's fine, but I'll take a look around and see if I spot anything unusual. With luck, he'll wander back in right when I'm elbow-deep in his underwear drawer."

"God forbid. Rose—"

"Yes?"

"Damon is awful. But awful or not, jerk or not, he's Sadie and Astrid's father. For their sake, I need to know where he is."

"I got it. Don't worry. I'm sure he'll turn up."

"I have to go."

"You go. See you later." I hung up.

Luella handed me my bag. "Let's go."

We pulled up to Izzy's like cops on a TV show, all screeching brakes and slamming doors. Inside, I greeted Braveheart and checked to make sure he had food and water before letting him out in Izzy's backyard.

Pepper hummed the melody of "Bad Moon Rising" while she flipped all the lights on one by one, as if Damon might pop out from a shadow.

I went down the hall to Damon's room and opened the door.

Luella and Pepper followed me in.

"Where would I have gone if I were Damon?" I picked up the condo brochures he'd collected on his dresser.

Pepper plucked a brochure from my hands and opened the accordion folds to full width. "We just destroyed the backyard a couple of days ago. You think he moved out to a condo already?"

"Maybe." I opened the closet. Luella and Pepper peered over my shoulder as I slid the hangers from one side to the other. "Nothing but clothing." I knelt and pulled out some boxes. "Nothing but shoes."

Pepper looked under the bed. "Nothing but dust bunnies."

Luella waited for Pepper to move, then plopped down on the bed. A strange expression came over her face. She gingerly touched the comforter. "Y'all …"

"What?" I said.

Luella stood up. "That bed is soaking wet!" She put her hands on her own rear. "Now *I'm* soaking wet!"

Pepper eyed the bed with undisguised horror. "You don't think he—"

Luella lifted her hands closer to her nose with a look of extreme reluctance. She sniffed. "It doesn't smell like anything."

We all exhaled.

"Still—I'm going to go wash my hands," she finished.

I lifted a corner of the blanket. It was heavy with water. "It's like he took a bath in here. Pepper, you're the water witch—can't you do something?"

She blinked. "Do something. Right." She raised her hands like an orchestra conductor, then dropped them to her sides. "Do what?"

Luella returned from washing her hands. "What are we doing?"

"Wait," said Pepper. "I got it. Can you get me a container?"

"What kind of container?" I asked.

"Like a bucket, or a jug."

I retrieved one of Izzy's recyclables from the kitchen.

Pepper took the empty jug and set it by her feet. "Let's see ..." Her tongue poked out from the corner of her lips as she concentrated. Tumbling silver eddies rolled from her extended hands. The magic spread over the wet comforter. One pinprick of moisture at a time, mist rose from the bed and coalesced into droplets above it.

"Ooh, a cloud!" said Luella.

Pepper brought her hands closer together, slowly, as if she were squeezing the air out of a beach ball. The cloud compacted into a wobbling sphere of water that floated between her hands. She made a twisting motion, and the water squished like clear dough into a tubular shape. The rope of water lengthened, thinned, and flowed neatly into the jug without a single drop going astray.

Pepper picked up the jug. "Ta-da!"

"That's great, Pepper," said Luella. "That water could have ruined the bed."

Pepper gave the jug a victory shake. "I'm a genius."

I frowned. I didn't feel like a genius at all. Surrounded by Damon's things, I had no idea where to find anything useful. Heat, mind reading, and hypnosis didn't do me any good in this situation. At least Pepper had accomplished something. "I wish Oliver was here."

"Ooh!" they chorused. Like schoolgirls.

"Shut up," I said. "I meant he seems to have relevant experience."

They looked at each other and grinned.

"Just what you need," said Pepper.

"Stop winking at me, Pepper, or I swear to God—"

This seemed to amuse them even more, so I turned away to rifle the dresser drawers in search of anything interesting. In the process of opening and closing the drawers, I dislodged the detritus on top of the dresser—and discovered a phone, which had been buried under an assortment of papers, notebooks, and magazines. "Look at this." I held it up. "No one goes anywhere without their phone these days."

"Call your sister," said Pepper. "Married people know each other's passwords."

"You don't think he changed it?"

Luella shook her head. "Dollars to doughnuts, he didn't bother."

I tapped out a message to Izzy on my own phone, but didn't press the send button. "Is this illegal or something? Not that I have a problem with doing it, but I prefer not to spend Christmas in jail for breaking into Damon's phone."

"Probably," said Pepper with a cheerful shrug.

"I think there are extenuating circumstances," said Luella. "I mean, isn't it natural to try to see if we can find out where he is? Even if that means looking at his phone? If we don't find something soon, the next step would be to get the police involved—and that would be more stressful for everyone. Including the kids."

"Good point, but it's probably better to talk about in person." I deleted the message to Izzy without sending it.

I picked up the jug and stared at the water inside like the sloshing liquid might reveal a secret. "Why on earth would he have poured water on the bed?"

Our mutual moment of silence was broken by the sound of Pepper's phone. She stared at the screen. "Queenie's calling an emergency meeting of all the witches for later today."

"Tell her we'll be there," I said.

25

Surfboards lined the walls of the Suntan Queen executive conference room like shields in a medieval hall. An oval wood table dominated the center of the space. "Not quite a Round Table," I mused.

"But close enough, darling." Queenie drifted past me in a cloud of perfume. She greeted Pepper with a European-style peck on each cheek, then took a seat at the head of the table.

Luella eyed the rolling leather chairs around the table. "Where should we sit?"

Queenie gestured with ring-covered fingers to the seat on her right. "Our guest will sit here. Your mother will sit next to her. Mrs. Millefleur and Oliver will be on my left."

Pepper frog-marched me toward Queenie's left. "Rose can sit here."

I dropped into the empty seat. Sitting was easier than arguing.

Pepper sat next to me. Luella took the chair on the other side of the table, next to where her mother would sit.

Mrs. Millefleur entered the room. She wore a royal purple suit jacket and skirt, and her hair was impeccably styled as usual. She swanned past me.

"Well, hello to you, too," I said.

Oliver followed and pulled out her chair, butler-like, before taking the seat next to mine. He rotated the chair to face me. "Good morning, Rose. I trust you rested well? Did your friends attend to your needs?"

"Yes, they did." His close attention made my breath come faster than it should have. My hand flew up to cover the quick rise and fall of my chest—then, realizing the motion only made his effect on me even more obvious, I pulled my hand away and tucked my hair behind my ear.

Why did I have to be such a wreck?

His eyes narrowed in thought. "I felt … responsible. I regret that I did not attend to you myself—but I didn't wish to impose."

The thought of Oliver *attending* to me didn't help my equilibrium.

Thankfully, the entrance of Mama saved me from further conversation. A woman accompanied her. Shock gripped me as I realized the newcomer was the fire dancer from the circus. She appeared to be about my age—I had assumed her to be much younger, but without the elaborate stage makeup, her true age revealed itself.

Queenie stood and came around the table. She patted Mama on the back and gave an affectionate double-cheek kiss to the fire dancer. "Tuesday, darling! It's been ages."

Pepper nudged me. "What's important about Tuesday? Did I miss something?"

"That's her name, I think. Not a day of the week."

"Ladies!" Queenie clapped her hands. "Oh, and gentlemen!" She acknowledged Oliver with a nod, then looked around. "Where's Raphael?"

"He couldn't leave work today," said Luella.

"Very well," said Queenie. "My dears, this is Tuesday. Tuesday is the lead witch at the Circus Aetherium, and we are lucky to be graced by her presence every so often here in Sparkle Beach."

Tuesday gave a little wave, and both of them sat down.

"Do we have a lead witch?" I whispered to Pepper.

She shrugged.

Queenie continued. "Why don't you tell us about what happened, Tuesday?"

The visitor sat forward. Sculpted finger waves tumbled around her face to form a bob that had been hidden by her elaborate headdress on the night of the performance. "Thank you, Queenie. We always love our stops at Sparkle Beach." Her eyes were large and expressive like a silent film star's, over high cheekbones that rounded when she smiled. "This time started like any other—we loaded out and checked our equipment, like we do before any show. There wasn't any worry about having to drum up business when we got here. We'd presold the tickets online; we're a small outfit, and we tend to sell out our performances. During the show, everything seemed to go like normal—until we got to the aerial part. The rest of us never go far from the ring during the show, so we were all nearby when it happened."

Tuesday looked down at her hands. A tiny flame bounced from finger to finger before she continued. "I felt a strange pull. Like someone tugging at my soul. It didn't feel good, let me tell you."

Mama patted Tuesday's arm. "Go on, girl."

Tuesday cast her a grateful look. "The pull flickered on and off. At first I thought it was just me. Then I saw that our aerialist was having trouble."

"Can she do her act without magic?" asked Luella.

Tuesday nodded. "She's a real aerialist. Her air magic is a safety mechanism, and a way of doing some more elaborate tricks than you might usually see. Anyway, I went running to the ring. So did everyone else. The tugging feeling got stronger. I heard a roar in my ears and I started to black out. And then she fell." Her gaze shifted to Oliver. "Queenie told me you saved her."

"Oliver is my bodyguard," interjected Mrs. Millefleur. "It is his job to protect others."

Tuesday raised eloquent, arching eyebrows. "Since when do you need a bodyguard? I don't remember you having one the last time I was here."

"That was a long time ago. Things have changed."

"Like what?" said Tuesday.

The exhaustion Mrs. Millefleur revealed the last time we met was gone. She could have been carved from marble—except for the intensity of her gaze, which went to each of us in turn. "I am a very private person, as most of you are aware—"

Mama let out an unladylike snort.

"Don't start with me, Belinda Campbell."

"Kiss my grits, Hilda Millefleur."

Tuesday looked back and forth between them. "When did you two stop getting along?"

Mama pointed at Mrs. Millefleur. "When she tossed my daughter and her boyfriend off a lighthouse."

Luella held her hand up for silence. "Mama, hang on a second. Mrs. Millefleur, you told me something was coming. Is this the 'something'? Why didn't you just tell us?"

Mama folded her arms over her chest and leaned back in her chair. "Because she's a *very private person*." The sarcasm was unmistakable.

If I didn't know better, I would have said there were hairline cracks in Mrs. Millefleur's marble facade. She was taking a slow breath—but trying to hide it—before speaking.

"Because this is a family matter," she said. "I wanted to handle it myself."

"You hired a bodyguard to protect you from your own family?" said Tuesday.

"From my sister."

Confusion flitted over Tuesday's face. "You never told me your sister was a witch."

"She is not a witch. She is a thief."

"And you thought it was a good idea to hide this from everyone?" said Mama.

Mrs. Millefleur slammed her hands on the table, her calm facade shattered. "She's *my* sister! *I* told her about my magic. *I* should have known better. *I* should have handled this in the first place. And now that she's capable of it, she's come back to take *all* of our magic, not just mine. All of it!"

"But if she's coming for all of us, why give me your magic?" I said. "What makes you think I can protect myself from your sister better than you can?"

She pinned me with a stare. "Because, Rose, you have a whole roomful of people to protect you." She waved a hand to indicate everyone else in the room. "You'll all band together and protect each other, like you do. And you won't have to worry about what happens to me, because I don't have any powers left to steal. I'm not even a witch anymore. I shouldn't even be here." She turned to Oliver. "Oliver, take me home. Then I will release you from your position. Your services are no longer needed."

Mama threw her head back and laughed. "Listen to you."

Mrs. Millefleur froze.

"Running out on everyone just because your sister turned out to be a thief. Don't you know every family has one of those? One of my cousins got arrested for trying to steal an alligator from Gatorland. You ain't special. You're just ashamed."

"I am not ashamed—"

"Yeah, you are. You're ashamed of your sister. You're ashamed you didn't stop her before. And now you think you're going to shut yourself in that fancy coquina house of yours and cry. Well, guess what? You're gonna help us stop her now, powers or no powers, before she steals anything else. You're gonna tell us everything you know, and then some. And then maybe, just maybe, I might begin to think about forgiving you for what you pulled with my Luella."

Silence fell.

Something about what Mrs. Millefleur had said nagged at me: *I should have handled this in the first place.*

Where had I heard something like that before? I closed my eyes. Winter days and nights sleeted backward in my mind: The circus. The sinkhole. Lovecats. The Christmas market.

The warehouse.

I can handle this my own way, she had said. To whom? Who was she talking to in the warehouse?

I groaned aloud as several realizations hit me at once.

"Rose?" said Luella.

"She's right," I said. "She shouldn't be here. She's been communicating with her sister all along."

26

I leaned in and caught Mrs. Millefleur's eye. "Admit it. You've been working with your sister all along."

Her mouth opened and closed.

"Rose—" Oliver interjected.

I faced him. "And how much did you know?"

"It's...complicated," he said.

We stared each other down.

Mrs. Millefleur laid a hand on his forearm. "Oliver," she said. "It's all right. I can defend myself."

Queenie steepled her fingers. The light glinted off the gems in her rings. "Rose, Oliver—stand down."

Oliver relaxed into his seat with calm self-possession.

I would deal with him later. I turned my attention to Queenie, who continued.

"Hilda, is this true? Have you betrayed us?"

"No." She took a deep breath and collected herself. "No. It's true—I met with Lenore at a downtown warehouse, as Rose guessed. But not for the reason you think."

"Enlighten us," Mama drawled.

"Lenore thinks I am working with her."

Several people around the table gasped.

"I am *not*," Mrs. Millefleur continued, "working with her. But it is to our advantage that she believes I am. I did not wish to tell you, because—"

"Because you're a very private person?" asked Mama, her voice filled with skepticism.

Mrs. Millefleur glared at her. "Because even I do not know what my sister is capable of. If she found a way to read your thoughts with her artifact, she would know I had betrayed her."

"Can she read minds?" said Pepper.

"I don't know what she can do. She does not reveal anything unless she has to."

"Apparently she's a very private person, too," said Mama.

"Your editorializing is entirely unnecessary, Belinda."

"Wait," I said. "What's an artifact?"

"They enhance, nullify, or store power. You have one," said Oliver. "The fire opal."

I fished it out from under my shirt. It was still warm from skin contact. "This?"

"Yes." He regarded me with an amused expression I didn't particularly like. "I made it."

"You—" I struggled to reconcile the twin urges that gripped me—one, to rip the thing off and throw it in his face; the other, to smugly tuck it back under my shirt.

Smug won out. "It's mine, now, isn't it?" I dropped the pendant and let it fall to its previous resting place. "Mrs. Millefleur gave it to me."

"Oh, it's *all* yours," he said. Underneath his cool demeanor, amusement still lurked.

All of a sudden, I wasn't so sure I'd made the right choice.

"How did she get an artifact in the first place?" Luella said.

"Stole it like a gator out of Gatorland," said Mama.

Pepper made a face like she was trying to work something out. "But if witches are all secretive about their powers, how did she find out where the magical people were so she could steal from them?"

Everyone looked at Mrs. Millefleur, who chose that moment to examine the wood grain on the table.

"Oh," said Pepper.

"I was young," said Mrs. Millefleur. "I was excited to share my newfound powers with someone. I never thought ..."

"Back to the point, darling." Queenie rested her chin in her hand. "What were you talking about in the warehouse?"

"She pressed me to honor our agreement."

"Which was?" said Mama.

"That I would give up my powers to her if she left the rest of the Sparkle Beach witches alone."

Pepper whistled.

Mrs. Millefleur glanced at me. "I told her my powers were too bound up with yours to release. That I needed more time."

"You were stalling. You thought you could find a way to stop her on your own," I said.

Mrs. Millefleur acknowledged the truth with a nod. "The attack on the Circus Aetherium— which would have been nominally under our protection while in Sparkle Beach— made it clear our agreement no longer stands."

"Lovely," said Tuesday.

Mama chuckled.

Mrs. Millefleur stared jets of fire across the table. "Does this amuse you?"

"You dumped your powers on Rose so your sister couldn't have the satisfaction of taking them from you, didn't you?" Mama's laughter became more pronounced. "Family! Can't live with 'em, can't shoot 'em."

Mrs. Millefleur waited for Mama's mirth to subside. "If there is one upside to 'dumping my powers,' as you say, it is that I no longer need Oliver to protect me."

Oliver sat up straight. "With all due respect, ma'am—"

"Oliver, she is no threat to me if I have nothing she wants."

His finely drawn lips came dangerously close to a pout, as if he were about to argue the point.

Mrs. Millefleur tapped the table to forestall him. "You must train Raphael. He needs a teacher. And you must protect Rose. Lenore is sure to target her."

"Who died and made you the lead witch?" said Mama.

Luella looked at the three elder witches. "Who *is* the lead witch?"

Queenie smiled faintly. "We are co-leads, your mother, Hilda, and I. At least, we were."

"Till one of us went rogue," added Mama.

Mrs. Millefleur puffed up like an agitated bird. "I am not rogue. I simply have a different approach."

Tuesday looked around the table with wide eyes. "I thought circus and theater people had the most drama—but you Sparkle Beach witches have us beat."

Queenie leaned back into her seat with a sigh. "Thank you, darling. It's nice to be number one at something."

Tuesday ignited her little flame again and bounced it from finger to finger. "I was hoping we could get some help to stage our make-up show." She extinguished the flame. "Because if we don't honor those tickets, that's our whole income gone—and a nasty mark on our reputation."

"I think you should go ahead and schedule your show," said Mama. "We'll provide the security."

Tuesday made a skeptical face. "What if the same thing happens?"

"We won't let it. We didn't know what was coming, last time. Now we do."

Luella looked at her mother. "No offense, Mama, but how are we going to make sure nothing happens?"

Tuesday lit up. "You could be part of the circus!"

"I've always wanted to join the circus," said Pepper. Then she visibly deflated. "But I can't. I have to take care of the kids."

"It's not a lifetime commitment," Tuesday said. "Just some rehearsal time and one show."

"You can swing that," I said to Pepper.

She brightened. "Yeah," she said, her voice becoming firm. "I can swing that."

Tuesday's gaze landed on me, and she raised her eyebrows. "Of course, you and I will have to be a double act."

I blinked. "What—me?"

She nodded.

"You want me to become a fire dancer on a day's notice?" Stage fright mixed with excitement set my stomach quaking.

"Like you said, it's just some rehearsal time and one show. We'll have to find you something to wear, too."

Visions of fire and spotlights danced in my head. "Do you have anything in black?"

27

After the meeting, I returned to Izzy's house. Since Damon had up and left, there was no reason to stay at Izzy's any longer. I slung the bag of dog food next to my small overnight satchel, ready to be loaded into the truck.

Sadie piped up from the doorway. "You leaving, Aunt Rose?" She padded into the room and hefted the bag of dog food. It looked comically large in her grip.

I gently tugged at the bag. "I'll take that, sweetheart."

Sadie gripped it tighter. "I got it. I'm very strong. Mommy says the Conleth women are all strong."

"Mommy says that?"

She nodded.

My eyes stung at the corners. Must have been Izzy's all-natural eco-friendly incense. "Your mommy says that because *her* mommy said that. Did you know that?"

"And her mommy was your mommy," Sadie said.

"Very true." I brushed at my eyes, then slung the satchel over my shoulder. "Now come on and let Aunt Rose help you carry that big old bag."

Sadie hesitated, clearly torn between proving her strength and sharing the burden.

"Sometimes it's okay to have help with a heavy load."

She considered this statement. Then a smile spread like sunshine over her face. She held out the bag.

I took a corner of it before the weight toppled her over. Together, we carried it to the truck and placed it in the cargo bed. I deposited my satchel in the cab, then followed Sadie back into the house.

Astrid had taken up residence on the couch, and was barely visible in a heap of quilts, a hooded jacket, and large headphones.

"Where's your mom?" I asked.

Astrid pulled off her headphones. "What?"

I repeated the question.

"Out back," she replied, and popped the headphones on.

I walked out the back door, where I had last seen Damon falling into a hole. The disturbed ground compacted under my feet with every step.

Izzy faced a gardening bench at the rear of the backyard, intent on some kind of work with various pots and cuttings.

"I'm heading out," I said.

She continued puttering with the plants. "We'll miss you."

"I'll be right down the road."

Izzy set down a pot and turned to face me. "You haven't told me what happened at the circus."

Mrs. Millefleur's words echoed in my mind: *I told her about my magic. I should have known better.*

I shook off the doubts—that was her sister, not mine—and told Izzy what had happened, from the night at the circus, to Mrs. Millefleur's house, to the surfboard-clad conference room at Suntan Queen. "And now I have to join the circus to protect the circus," I finished. I studied her face. Was she envious? Relieved? Indifferent?

She hugged me before I knew what hit me. "Promise me you'll be careful, Rose."

"Who needs careful? Conleth women are strong."

Izzy released me from the hug, then held me at arms length and shook me. "Strong, yes. Invincible, no. Don't do anything stupid."

"I promise not to do anything stupid. Satisfied?"

She reached for a small clay pot. "Here, take this. For luck."

"Izzy, you know about me and plants—"

"Smell it."

I raised an eyebrow and took the pot. It smelled of Thanksgivings long past. "What is it?"

"Sage. Overall good vibes and wisdom."

"Not if I kill it."

"Well, then you can burn it and wave the smoke around."

I laughed at that. "All right, if you insist." I tucked the pot in the crook of my arm. "Oh, and let me know when you hear from Damon."

"I looked at his phone, like you suggested. Nothing out of the ordinary."

"I'm sure he's fine," I said, "but when you worry, I worry."

"I'll keep you posted."

We parted, Izzy to her plants and I to collect Braveheart. I buckled him securely into his harness and shoved the pot in a cup holder. Braveheart sniffed at the sage, then sneezed.

"Time to go," I said. "But first, I need my kitty sidekick. Horatio!"

Horatio appeared on the narrow middle seat between Braveheart and me. He settled Sphinx-like on the vinyl and flexed his claws into the material.

I took one hand off the wheel to scratch his warm little head, then I threw the truck into reverse. "Let's roll."

We arrived in short order at the cabin, which sat lonely in the middle of the woods, looking for all the world as if it had been sulking in my absence. I grabbed an armload of firewood on my way in. Once inside, I arranged the wood and blasted it into a cheery fire to take the chill out of the air. Braveheart galloped happily into the backyard, and Horatio took up his usual post curled at the base of the fire.

I flopped on the couch. "Home sweet home," I said. "Alone at last." After a moment with my feet up, the satisfaction waned. I should have been blissed out to the max to finally have my life to myself. Instead, a restless energy snaked through my limbs. I turned this way and that, trying to get comfortable enough to relax.

I took out my phone and attempted to distract myself by scrolling through pictures of elaborate recipes I would never cook. The digital parade of colorful macarons, hulking beef Wellingtons, and giant pans of paella failed to soothe me for even ten seconds. I put the phone down in disgust. What was wrong with me?

Horatio uncurled from the coals and stalked across the living room. He leaped onto the couch and made himself comfortable on my stomach.

"Bored, Horatio. I'm bored." I patted his back and he rumbled into a full-blown purr. "Too much excitement lately. I need to slow down and act my age."

Horatio regarded me with solemn golden eyes.

It was like looking into a mirror. A judgy little cat mirror. "Don't look at me like that." I sighed. "Fine. I give up trying to be sedate." I sat up, sending him leaping off my stomach and onto the floor.

He gave me a severe stare before stalking away out of sight.

I snatched up my phone. "I'll bug Oliver. He deserves a little stress after pulling that stunt at the meeting today." I bit my lip as I formulated a message. *If you ever tell me 'It's complicated' again, I swear I'll singe your nose hairs.* Reading it aloud, it sounded a bit too flirty, considering I'd meant it to sound threatening.

Oh, well.

I hit the send button.

My grooming is already immaculate, he replied. *But thank you for the kind offer.*

"Kind offer my—" I stabbed at the keys to type a reply: *I want a timeline and an explanation for what you knew and when you knew it.*

I could almost hear the laughter in his response. *Are you always this demanding?*

Usually I'm worse, I replied.

Where are you? he wrote.

Home.

Are you alone? Would you be willing to try something?

My brow knitted. What was he up to? I wrote back a single word: *Maybe.*

Put down your phone and hold the necklace.

Caution evaporated in the wake of excitement. Magic was becoming an exhilaration and a hunger I couldn't deny. I wrapped my hand around the fire opal and waited.

The stone thrummed beneath my touch. A glow leaked from between my fingers.

Rose. Oliver's voice vibrated through my bones. *Can you hear me?* It wasn't like Luella's or Mama's telepathy, which buzzed in my ear like a bee. This was like slow, deep waves that shook me on a molecular level.

I gripped the stone tighter. "I hear you. Can you hear me?"

Yes. A pause. *This is so much better than texting, don't you think?*

"Your voice shakes me. Does mine do the same to you?" I meant it as an academic question, but somehow it came out all wrong.

Without a doubt, he said.

My mouth went dry. Time for a subject change. "So tell me about Mrs. Millefleur's sister. Lenore."

Mrs. Millefleur has been holding Lenore at bay for some time. When she suspected that her sister might be close to reneging on their bargain, she hired me. Although I insist that my clients disclose all pertinent information, Mrs. Millefleur can be—as you know—on the reticent side. I knew she was in touch with her sister. I did not know they were meeting face-to-face. Nor would I have permitted such a meeting, if I had known.

I snorted. "As if Mrs. Millefleur would have cared whether you 'permitted' anything or not."

True.

I considered his words and idly rubbed the fire opal with my thumb.

Oliver gasped, sending a pulse of shock across our connection. *That tickles, Rose.*

The heat on my face went all the way to the tips of my ears—and it wasn't from the cozy fire I'd laid.

28

The morning of the next day filled me with so much anticipation I couldn't help arriving early at the fairgrounds for my scheduled practice session. The circus tent pennants flapped in a brisk breeze, but Horatio on my shoulders served as a warming barrier against the wind.

I crossed the sandy parking lot and entered the tent through the open flap.

Tuesday crouched over an array of metal frames laid out on the floor. She stood with fluid grace, tugged an attached skirt back into alignment with her black yoga pants, and smoothed out her matching black tank top. When she noticed me, she raised a hand in greeting. "Great minds think alike," she said, nodding to my outfit.

I'd donned my favorite Ouija board yoga capris and a moon phase top—in black, of course.

Tuesday smiled as she approached, but she wasn't looking at me anymore. She had eyes only for Horatio. "Who's this fuzzy friend?"

"This is Horatio," I said. I reached up and gave him a scratch behind the ears.

"Can I hold him?"

"I'm … not sure? Can you?"

"Sure, if you permit it—and he goes along with it."

I coaxed Horatio into my arms. "He's a little stubborn, and a little proud—but pretty cuddly when it comes right down to it."

Tuesday reached out. I carefully laid Horatio in her arms.

"Isn't he lovely," she said.

Horatio blinked his golden eyes and seemed nonplussed.

"You're the first person to hold him. My sister was able to pet him briefly, though."

"Is she a witch?" Tuesday smoothed her hand over Horatio's fur.

"No. Just me."

"How'd you do it?"

I explained how I'd used fire magic hypnosis to help Izzy see Horatio.

Tuesday's eyebrows rose. "What a cool idea." She shifted to offer Horatio to me.

I took him back into my arms.

"There's someone I want you to meet," she said. "Spiral!" At Tuesday's call, a cat appeared at her feet. This cat was deep orange mixed with white. The orange and white swirled into a perfect spiral pattern on the cat's flank. "Come here,

Spiral, you great big marmalade pudding." She scooped the cat up. "She's a fire cat, too."

I examined Spiral. Like Horatio, her tail was fire-tipped. Her eyes appeared golden at first glance, but upon closer inspection, were more like the golden orange hue of the gem I wore around my neck. "She's gorgeous."

Horatio's whiskers twitched. Clearly he was doing his own evaluation.

"I didn't see Spiral during your act the other night," I said.

"She doesn't usually come out for shows. Having her around is kind of like splitting your mind into two places." Tuesday smiled down at the cat. "You can pet her. She loves fire witches."

I petted the orange cat. "Her fur radiates warmth just like Horatio's."

"Fire witch familiars will have things in common, like fire witches do, but each one is unique."

"Can I ask you something?"

"Fire away. Ha! Just a little fire humor for you."

"What should I do with Horatio during practice? I've never sent him away before. He just wanders off when he feels like it, and I summon him when I want him."

"Try setting him down." Tuesday lowered her familiar to the ground.

I followed suit with Horatio.

The two cats touched noses. Spiral let out an inquisitive meow.

Tuesday eyed the cats. "I think they'll keep each other occupied while we get to work. How about I show you the props?"

We moved to the center of the ring where the frames lay on the ground. I recognized the oval frame from the performance, but there were several other shapes and a pair of metal wings I hadn't seen in use.

"I thought we'd keep it simple, since we don't have a lot of time to prepare, and I want you to be able to keep your mind on alert for threats. If I load you up with choreography you'll be concentrating on that." She picked up the wing frame. "I was thinking maybe you could wear these and sort of pose as a background dancer. That keeps you in range to notice if anything seems amiss during my performance."

I took the wings from her grasp and hefted them. "Not too heavy," I said.

Tuesday took the wings and laid them aside. "Let's get your hair out of the way." She swiftly bound my hair into a bun and pinned it securely in place with bobby pins from a hidden pocket. "Your fire magic can stop fires from happening, but there's no point in taking chances and accidentally setting your hair on fire. We have magic, but we prepare as if we don't." She plucked at my tank top. "What percentage cotton is this? How about your pants?"

"Um …"

"Never mind, I'll look." She pulled the tag up from the back of the shirt, then deftly flipped the back of my waistband to reveal the garment tag. "Both ninety-seven percent. Not bad. You need a mostly natural fabric. Synthetic fabrics melt when they burn, and you don't want to see what that does to skin."

I made a valiant attempt to wipe the horrified grimace off my face.

"Don't worry, you'll be fine." She stepped back and gave me a full body once-over. "And it has to be snug, too. No fringe or lace or frippery. This will be fine for practice. We'll get you something fancy out of the costume trunk later."

"Are you sure I should be handling live fire for the show?"

Tuesday let out a hearty laugh. "Are you kidding? I'm not letting you handle fire. This is just the safety precautions for being *near* the fire."

Relief flooded through me. "I mean, it looks like fun, but—"

She thumped me on the back, clearly amused by my reaction. "Dancers train for ages before they light up. I want you to be close enough to sense any spells aimed at me, but that doesn't mean you have to spin fire while you do it."

"What about the fire wings?"

Tuesday lifted the frame and pointed to several brackets I hadn't noticed before. "See these? We can fit these with LED lights. Works like magic ... well, almost." She set the wings down. "I'll be doing my usual routine."

She walked me through the marks and musical cues, mostly so I would know how to stay out of the way, and then had me attempt several basic dance moves.

Basic for Tuesday, anyway.

"It's simple," she said. "Lift the hip, drop the hip. Like this." She bounced her right hip in a jaunty motion.

I tried it. My hip did not appreciate trying to move independently of the rest of my skeleton. It probably looked like I was having a spasm. "I'm sorry," I said. "I promise you, I *can* dance—these moves are just a little different than what I'm used to."

"No problem, no problem," said Tuesday. "We'll figure this out." She paced in front of me, then snapped her fingers. "Try this. Maybe something smoother will be easier." She dipped and raised each hip in turn with a sinuous ice cream-scooping motion.

I attempted to replicate the snaky movement.

Tuesday's face told me everything I needed to know about how I was doing.

I covered my face with my hands. "I can't do this. I can't be onstage with you."

"Don't get discouraged. Arms! We'll try arms." She lifted her arms to the positions of noon and three o'clock, transforming her posture into a graceful dancer's carriage.

I dutifully copied the position. It was, indeed, easier than the hips.

"Now roll your hand like this. Like scooping the last of the peanut butter out of the jar."

I mirrored her.

"Yes! That's great! Now bring your arm down while you're doing it—slowly, slowly—good."

I completed the movement and let my arms drop to my sides. "Was that okay?"

"It was *very* good."

I suspected she was protecting my feelings as if I were a small child. "Tuesday, I don't want to make a mess of your act, or make a fool of myself—"

"Stop fretting. All we need are four eight-counts. Then you can repeat it." She did a double take. "You know what an eight-count is, right?"

"A count of eight?" I said in the driest voice I could muster.

"Sassy." Tuesday gave my upper arm a backhanded slap. "You're such a fire witch." Her attention shifted to something over my shoulder that made her eyes widen. "Oh, look out—here comes trouble."

I turned to find Raphael and Oliver approaching the ring.

"Hey, ladies," said Raphael with a friendly wave. "How's it going?" His blue jeans and plaid flannel shirt contrasted with Oliver's black sweater and slacks.

Tuesday smirked. "Going for the beatnik look, Oliver?"

"Hello, Tuesday. I see your razor-sharp wit hasn't lost its keen edge." His gaze shifted to me. "Rose."

With a single glance and a single word from Oliver, every interaction we'd had flashed across my mind like sparks off a saw. Damn him. "Hello, Oliver." Then I realized I'd wrapped my hand around the fire opal pendant. I quickly let it go and tried to look casual.

"Are you practicing?" asked Raphael.

"Can we watch?" added Oliver, with an air of nonchalance.

Tuesday opened her mouth to respond, but I cut her off. "Not on your life. You can watch when everybody else does. During the show." Only then did I allow my gaze to shift back to Tuesday. "Right, Tuesday?"

She looked back and forth between Oliver and me, her large eyes making the movement eloquent. "Right …"

I dusted my hands. "That's settled, then."

Oliver briefly studied his fingernails. "I don't mind if *you* watch, though."

"But we're not done yet—" I began.

"Goody!" said Tuesday, right over my objection. "Come on, Rose." She steered me to the stands and practically shoved me onto the nearest bench.

29

A raccoon ran into the ring. Raphael scooped up the chunky mischief-maker and nuzzled her masked face. "Who's Daddy's little princess?" he said.

Oliver froze like he'd been cast in bronze. "*What* is that?"

"This is Princess," said Raphael. He held the raccoon's paw and made a waving motion. "Say hello to the nice man, Princess."

Oliver sighed. "Do you think you could send it away for now?"

The raccoon looked offended. So did Raphael. "It?" he said.

"Her," amended Oliver.

Horatio and Spiral dashed into the ring. They milled around Raphael's feet, making meows of curiosity—then they sat and stared at Oliver with casual feline insolence.

Oliver made an exasperated noise. "What is this, a menagerie?"

I nudged Tuesday and lowered my voice. "Does he not have a familiar?"

"Oh, he's got one," said Tuesday. "But he's old school. Doesn't believe in letting your familiar run around willy-nilly."

"I heard that," Oliver said. "It's a security risk. If you let your familiar accompany you at all times, other witches will instantly know what you are. You'll never be able to pass undetected."

"Relax, Oliver," I said. "You're among friends."

A strange look passed over his face, something between longing and discomfort, and was gone before I was even sure I'd seen it.

"We have work to do," he said. He turned away from the stands, toward Raphael, effectively ending the conversation

Raphael set Princess on the ground. She scuttled away under the stands, followed by Horatio and Spiral.

Oliver addressed Raphael. "Before you can use any protective magic, you need to be able to see threats coming in the first place. Stand here." He indicated the center of the ring. "Close your eyes. Magic is easier without multitasking, at least until you get the hang of it."

Raphael moved into position and closed his eyes.

"I'm going to reach out with my own magic from different locations inside the tent. See if you can point to where the magic is coming from."

"Couldn't he just open his eyes and look for the magic?" I asked. "It's silver, like the fire on the end of Horatio's tail."

"If a witch is in sight, you may see their magic in action—but what if they're around a corner? You must rely on sensing it." Oliver retreated with quiet footsteps until he stood almost at the main entrance to the tent. He raised one hand toward Raphael. Silver glitter dripped like sand from his fingers.

While this was going on, Princess crept out from under the stands and watched Oliver with bright, inquisitive eyes.

Raphael moved his arm like a compass needle near a magnet, swaying from left to right until he stopped and pointed in Oliver's direction with confidence. "There."

Oliver lowered his hand, and the magic dissipated. He silently moved to a spot behind Raphael.

Princess darted from one hiding place to another to follow Oliver. Then, she snuck around behind him.

Oliver raised his hand. Again, silver glitter fell.

With his eyes still closed, Raphael slowly turned in a circle until he got a bearing on Oliver. His arm rose just as Princess bolted forward and sank her teeth into Oliver's ankle.

"Bloody hell!" Oliver whipped around in time to see Princess dash away through a gap in the tent flaps. "She bit me!"

Raphael opened his eyes, a look of confusion on his face. "Who bit you?"

"Your bandit familiar, that's who." Oliver leaned down and examined the punctures in his trousers.

"Can she do that?"

"Of course she can. They can have physical presence if they choose. Ow," he added.

"Hey, Oliver," I said, "if you can sense magic, shouldn't you have seen that coming?"

Chagrin flitted across his face. "If I hadn't been concentrating on Raphael, I would have. This is a prime example of why witches shouldn't multitask if they can possibly avoid it." He cocked his head. "Let's try that again. Raphael, see if you can get your little monster to charge me."

"Hey, now, that's my Princess you're talking about," said Raphael.

Oliver pressed his hands to his forehead, as if saying a prayer for patience. "Can you get your little Princess to charge me?"

"Are you sure you can handle the smackdown?"

Oliver made a get-on-with-it gesture.

Raphael shrugged. "It's your leg."

I smiled and leaned in. This show was so good, I needed a bucket of popcorn.

Raphael concentrated, but said nothing aloud.

This surprised me. Although I spoke to Horatio all the time, I hadn't *thought* at him very often—not intentionally, at least. It was something I would have to experiment with.

Princess poked her nose through the gap between the tent flaps. She sniffed in the direction of Raphael, then Oliver, as if assessing the distance. She sprang from her hiding place and charged Oliver.

The dirt floor adjacent to Oliver shifted.

Princess skidded to a stop and held one front paw off the ground.

A silver sand-like substance boiled from the shifting earth—then exploded upward. Dust flew into the air.

When it cleared, a shaggy-haired brown bear stood in the circus ring. Its brown eyes, the color of chocolate diamonds, shone in the overhead lights. The bear shook itself, sending dirt flying in all directions. It turned its gaze to Princess and regarded the raccoon with something like long-suffering tolerance.

My jaw dropped. Whatever I had been expecting Oliver's familiar to be, it wasn't this.

Raphael ran to interpose himself between the bear and the raccoon. "Don't you dare hurt my Princess."

"Calm down. They can't harm each other." Oliver approached the bear and laid a hand on its back. "This is Arthur." He walked in front of the bear and knelt on the floor, putting his head nearly level with the bear's. His hands cupped the bear's face. "Arthur, let's show these witches how it's done, shall we?"

The bear made a chuffing sound.

Oliver relaxed into a deep kneeling position with his hands behind his back.

The bear reared back and raised one massive paw tipped with five sharp claws.

My hand went to my mouth.

Arthur swung his paw straight at Oliver's face—and it passed through harmlessly, like a mirage.

I gasped. "I thought he was going to take your face off."

"We'll be adding you to the circus before you know it, Oliver," said Tuesday.

Oliver smiled, seeming simultaneously pleased and perhaps a little embarrassed by the fuss. He got to his feet and made a very neat bow followed by a sweeping gesture to Arthur.

Arthur went on his hind legs and offered a bearish bow, then dropped down to stand on four legs again.

Tuesday, Raphael, and I all clapped.

"As you can see," said Oliver, "they are perfectly capable of being solid or insubstantial. If one familiar were to take a swipe at another, the intended victim could phase out and be unharmed. Unfortunately," he added, looking down at his ankle, "we witches cannot do the same."

I couldn't resist any longer. I hopped down from the stands and approached the brown bear. "Can I pet him?"

"Of course," he said.

I sank my fingers into the thick fur at the scruff of the bear's neck. The fur shed glimmers of silver when I combed my fingers down his back. "He's majestic."

"He is King Arthur, indeed," said Oliver.

"Hello, your majesty," I said to the bear. "Now we have a Princess—and a king."

Arthur sank to his hindquarters and leaned his shaggy head against me.

I staggered from the weight. "Wow. He's heavy enough when he wants to be."

Horatio padded out with hesitant steps from underneath the stands, followed by Spiral. They looked at each other, then stared at the large brown bear.

Princess peeked out from where she'd hidden behind Raphael.

"It's all right," I said to the familiars. "The big bear won't hurt you. He's a friend."

As if to prove the point, Arthur flopped to the ground like a lumpy rug with two-inch claws.

I concentrated on sending out soothing vibes. A calm presence affected animals; why not familiars, too?

Horatio raised his chin and stalked boldly over to Arthur. He curled up against Arthur's massive shoulder and lashed his tail in a saucy fashion.

Spiral approached the bear next. She settled against the side of Arthur's fuzzy belly and groomed herself as if she hadn't a care in the world.

Princess dashed around Raphael and scrambled onto the bear's back. She stretched out comfortably along his spine. Then she used her front paws to grab handfuls of bear fur as if they were reins.

It made for an unusual tableau—a bear, two cats, and a raccoon, all in one furry pile.

Oliver's eyebrows rose. "How did you do that?"

"Do what?"

"You told Arthur not to present a threat. You told the other familiars not to be afraid, and they listened."

I shrugged. "They're animals, aren't they? I train animals."

"Not like this, you don't. No one ever has." His keen eyes regarded me with a new and assessing expression. "Until now."

It was then that I noticed how the familiars' gemlike gazes had fallen on me—as if they were awaiting my next command.

30

After a full day of training with the witches of the Circus Aetherium, Luella, Pepper, and I retreated to Luella's cozy shotgun house on the beach side of town.

Pepper sprawled on the couch. Her shiny mermaid-patterned tights—a gift from the circus water witches—sparkled in the twinkling lights of the old-fashioned Christmas tree in the corner of the living room. "No one ever told me the circus was so much work," she said.

Luella entered the living room with a tray of cookies. "Poor Pepper," she said, in an affectionately teasing tone. "Have a cookie."

Pepper scooped up four snowflake-shaped cookies from the tray. "You'd need cookies, too, if you spent the day hauling water around while two water witches try to get you to drop it."

"Mama and I had to practice catching falling objects until I thought I was going to pull some kind of magical muscle. So I see your cookies and raise you one," said Luella. She chose five cookies and set the tray on the coffee table before taking a seat.

"I was literally putting out fires all day." I eyed the tray. "How many cookies do I get?"

"Didn't you do something with the familiars, too? Raphael said Oliver was all shook up," said Luella.

I smiled to myself at the thought of Oliver being all shook up. Then I told the story in its entirety to Luella and Pepper.

"You deserve *all* the cookies," said Pepper. "That's impressive."

I took a cookie and nibbled it. The sugary, buttery bite melted in my mouth, leaving behind a sweet vanilla flavor. "Do you feel ready for this? For the performance, I mean— and being responsible for it going off without a hitch."

Luella smoothed her braid. Her face took on a thoughtful expression. "Between Mama and me, I feel like we can handle whatever comes up. Although I admit: I'm nervous."

"Pepper?" I asked.

"I say bring it on. We may not have been ready last time, but this time …" She trailed off and posed with her hands in a magician's conjuring position.

I dusted the crumbs off my fingers, then ignited a little dancing flame like Tuesday had at our meeting. I bounced it from fingertip to fingertip, above nails I had recently painted with black and silver flames. "Tuesday has a water witch standing by as a spotter. I'm just there to watch for unexpected fire magic. I think I can handle that."

Pepper laced her hands behind her head. "What did she say to do if you saw any?"

"First I warn Tuesday and her spotter. Then I try to absorb it with this artifact." I lifted the fire opal pendant and let it fall. "Earth magic can have a dampening effect on fire. That's why it helped when Mrs. Millefleur decided to unload her leftover powers on me. Meanwhile, I have to parade around in metal wings and try to look like I belong onstage."

"Mama and I are doing something similar," said Luella. "Except we're the air magic spotters, and Oliver will be on hand with a soft landing if there's an air magic failure. Raphael will also be on alert for rogue earth magic."

In the quiet that followed, Zephyr and Horatio emerged from the hallway, fresh from some unknown adventure.

Luella held out her arms. "Here, girl!"

Zephyr bounded to Luella. Horatio, on the other hand, regally approached the Christmas tree and began investigating the lower branches.

Luella ruffled Zephyr's silver-white fur. "You should try calling her," she said.

"Calling her?"

"Like you did at the circus with the other familiars," said Pepper. She rolled on her side on the couch, to watch.

"Here, Zephyr," I said. Zephyr trotted over in a friendly fashion and looked up at me with ice-blue eyes. I petted her soft fur, which gave off an ineffable warm breeze at all times.

"I don't know that this proves anything. I mean, any witch could call her, couldn't they?"

"*Think* a command," said Luella. "Raphael does it with Princess all the time."

Not to be outdone by Raphael, I concentrated on the first command that popped into my mind: *Fly to the top of the Christmas tree.*

Zephyr cocked her head. Then she took off from a standing start. She ran up the side of the tree, ruffling the needles as she went. When she reached the top, she hovered above the silver star and looked pleased with herself.

Pepper sat straight up on the couch. "Did you tell her to run up the tree?"

I nodded.

"Well, I'll be," said Luella. "Down, Zephyr."

The dog glided to the floor.

Horatio ignored Zephyr and batted at a low-hanging ornament.

"Too bad cats aren't as cooperative as dogs," I said.

Pepper snorted. "Rose, Horatio's *your* familiar. He's *just like you*. Haven't you noticed that yet?"

"He is not like me. He's stubborn, touchy, and—oh. I stand corrected."

"Are we all similar to our familiars?" Luella's brow furrowed. "What on earth does Raphael have in common with a raccoon named Princess?"

Pepper laughed.

"Think about it," I said. "Princess is mischievous, but she's affectionate and protective, too. Remind you of anyone?"

A fond smile lit up Luella's face, along with a hint of color.

"But what about Oliver?" said Pepper. "His familiar let two cats and a raccoon use him as a fur-covered space heater. What does that mean?"

Luella met my gaze. "I bet it's because underneath that cool exterior, Oliver's a big old softy."

"So *that's* why he's shy of showing off that bear," said Pepper.

My cheeks heated. "I think it's because of the risk to operational security—"

"Operational security, my hind leg," said Luella, sounding very much like her mother. "Of course that's the 'reason,' but it's also a convenient way of not letting anyone know what a cuddly critter you are when you want to be perceived as too cool for school." She gave me a pointed look.

I pretended not to notice.

Pepper sat forward on the couch as if something had occurred to her. "Hey, you don't think Mrs. Millefleur's sister—what was her name?"

"Lenore," I said.

"Lenore. You don't think Lenore might have some artifact that would help my familiar show up, do you?"

"It seems unlikely," I said. "She's not a witch, so she couldn't have a familiar even if she wanted one; therefore, why would she have an artifact related to familiars? And how would we get it?"

Pepper slumped. "Yeah, I guess that's true."

Luella reached over and patted Pepper on the back. "Don't worry. Your time will come."

I scooted closer. It wasn't like Pepper to get so discouraged. "Come on. We're the Ride-or-Die Witches. We can do anything, including finding MIA familiars." To my ears, it sounded like I was grasping at straws—but Pepper cast me a look of hope.

"You think?" she said.

"Sure," I replied, with as much hearty reassurance as I could put on. When Pepper looked away, I locked eyes with Luella, silently urging her to go with it.

"Rose is right," said Luella. "If anyone can figure it out, it's us."

"Pepper," I said, "remember when my magic first manifested and I couldn't stop blasting fire?"

"Yeah," said Pepper, smiling at the memory. "I was sure you were going to toast the interior of my SUV."

"But I didn't, right? It worked out."

She nodded slowly.

"This will too."

Pepper grabbed my hand and gave it a squeeze. "You know, for someone who wears all black and listens to The Cure on repeat, you're actually pretty positive."

"Don't tell anyone," I said. "You'll ruin my image."

31

Saturday turned unseasonably warm, causing me to sweat lightly under my borrowed costume while we prepared for the evening's show. The more the sun sank toward the horizon, the more the sweat cooled. By the time the moon rose, I shivered, and my stomach trembled. It was hard to tell what was nerves and what was a chill.

I straightened the tights that disappeared into my boots and fluffed the skirt attached to the black leotard. I retrieved the sage leaf I'd brought in my bag, then rolled it up and pinned it discreetly under my neckline for good luck. With my costume ready for the performance, I peeked out from backstage to watch the crowd trickle into the tent.

Several Sparkle Beach witches were already out front, including Mrs. Millefleur, who stood at the entrance in an outfit that combined a scarlet business suit with a jaunty majorette's hat. She looked like she was on her way to a

Downtown Merchants' Guild costume party. She would collect tickets—and be on the lookout for Lenore.

Queenie took her position at a card table off to the side, under a hastily created banner that read "The Amazing Queenie." Her fortune-teller's costume suited her all the way from its feathered turban down to the hem of the patchwork silk robe. A large glass tip jar sat prominently on the table. With her unique ability to read moods, Queenie would keep an eye on the crowd.

I sensed heat behind me, and let the backstage curtain fall shut before I turned.

It was Oliver.

He wore a black ringmaster's costume trimmed with gold. The costume gave him a melancholy grace, like an old-fashioned daguerreotype come to life. He removed his black top hat. "Well met, fire witch."

"Good evening." The night had an air of seriousness that wrapped both of us in its embrace. There was no need to smooth my already snug-fitting costume, but I did so anyway, tugging the sweetheart neckline here and there beneath the fire opal pendant.

"I wanted to wish you good—" he began.

"Don't say it." I laid a hand on his arm. "Tuesday told me to use 'break a leg.'"

Oliver gave a rueful chuckle. "My mistake. Break a leg, Rose."

I smiled. "Break a leg, earth witch."

He hesitated—then leaned forward and brushed my cheek with a kiss as soft and warm as falling ash.

I touched my cheek. "What was that for?"

"For—" He paused. "For what I couldn't say." He replaced his top hat and walked away.

I hadn't decided whether he meant luck, or something else, when I caught Pepper looking at me from across the room. She made an exaggerated double thumbs up and launched into some kind of impromptu celebratory dance.

Tuesday's approach cut off my view of Pepper's victory shuffle. She inspected my costume, including the French hood and caul covering my hair, and applied a few judicious adjustments. "We're up first. Are you ready?"

My stomach flip-flopped. "I'm ready," I said, making an effort to sound convincing. I stepped in front of the mirror positioned near the curtain for one last look at myself. The combination of the black headpiece, leotard, and leggings made me look like a fairy ballerina of the night—if fairy ballerinas of the night favored black suede boots over dainty slippers.

Tuesday's spotter entered the ring before the opening fanfare for a final check and to take a position near the stage.

Tuesday lifted the wing frame, strapped it to my back, and flicked each of the LEDs to life.

I took slow breaths to calm my racing heart.

When our musical cue sounded, someone held the curtain aside. I stepped through and entered the ring like Tuesday had shown me, all slow steps and graceful gestures to accompany the music. The crowd generated a collective warmth around me, but with the lights in my eyes, I could see nothing but silhouettes.

A flare in my peripheral vision revealed Tuesday coming in behind me. I continued my circuit of the ring until

I reached the back of it. Once I reached my mark, I struck the first pose.

In the front of the ring, Tuesday began her performance.

I could only devote half my attention to the whirling flames in front of me. I reached my awareness around the ring, alert for the intrusion of fire magic that didn't belong to Tuesday or me. I moved through the first combination we'd rehearsed—grapevine steps to the right, lotus hands, snake hips—then repeated the whole thing to the left.

The next combination was more complicated, and I almost stumbled on one of the three-step turns, but I managed to glide into the next pose without embarrassing myself too much.

Time flowed fast and slow simultaneously. The constant alertness for magic sapped my strength more than I expected. Before I knew it, Tuesday had extinguished her flames, and the approval of the audience roared in my ears. Together, we ran backstage to make way for the next performers.

"Did you feel anything?" said Tuesday. She unstrapped the wings.

Breath eluded me as I tried to come down from the adrenaline high of being onstage. I shook my head. "Nothing." Although I wanted to stay at the curtain and catch some of the acts I'd missed the first time around, I only managed to peek out and catch a moment or two of the juggling act before I had to go help Pepper finish getting ready.

Pepper sat at a small folding table with a propped-up mirror. A tiny garland of string lights draped the frame. In the dim illumination, she was having trouble putting the finishing touches on her own makeup. "This is not my thing," she said, handing the makeup bag to me with an apologetic grimace.

I assessed her progress. True to form, she'd gone way too light on the eyeshadow and the blush. If she went onstage like that, she'd be completely washed out. "Don't move," I said.

Pepper shimmied in her seat before going still.

I wielded the blue and green eyeshadows with liberal swipes to match her iridescent fish-scale outfit. Her cheeks got an unnatural helping of pink until they glowed like apples in season. A thick application of glittery green lipstick finished the look.

Pepper checked my work in the little mirror. "Oof," she said. "Does it have to be so ... bright?"

"Yes."

Pepper stuck her bright green bottom lip out.

"Don't move. We have to get your headpiece on."

The finishing touch was a confection of a crown, covered with gems and coral bits and draped with dangling pearl strands. I lowered it over her curls and secured it with a dozen bobby pins.

Pepper touched it carefully while turning her head this way and that in front of the mirror. "Look at me! I'm queen of the mermaids."

"Come on, queen of the mermaids. You're up." I accompanied her to the curtain and handed her a prop sceptre made of driftwood and covered with shells and silver sequins. We peeked out in time to see a handful of Circus Aetherium witches rapidly rolling out what looked like an oversized pop-up kiddie pool. Whatever it was, I hadn't seen it in the first show, or during the practice session. "Break a fin," I said.

But Pepper was already somewhere else, mentally speaking. A serious look had descended on her face. She bounced on the balls of her feet with barely contained energy. She pushed the curtain aside and entered the ring.

Dual blasts of water, seemingly from nowhere, filled the pool in seconds. Pepper posed at the back of the pool while the other two water witches glided across the water. Whereas Pepper looked like a mermaid queen, the circus witches resembled strange sea creatures with ropes of kelp-like hair and mottled silver scales for skin.

They appeared to walk on water, at first—which was more than enough to fascinate the crowd—and then they opened their mouths to sing.

Music from the sound system ceased, and all that could be heard was the sound, somehow both drifting and piercing, of the witches' song. Crystalline drops of water rose from the pool and spread outward carrying the tune like tiny amplifiers.

The song of the sea flowed like a tide of memory. In the midst of it stood Pepper with a faraway look on her face. I could only hope that her concentration remained firm under the influence of the siren song.

The two water witches spun and leaped across the surface of the water like it was made of ice. They brought the song to its eerie, reverberant conclusion with the rapid implosion of the drifting droplets. The sphere of gathered water hung in the air before dropping with a splash into the pool below. With a theatrical gesture from all three witches, the water fountained away and disappeared. They took their bows and ran backstage.

In the darkness that fell, the perfectly dry pop-up pool was rolled up and removed.

Luella and Mama jogged past, their riotously colored feathered headdresses bouncing, as they followed the aerialist into the ring.

Oliver, in his ringmaster suit, and Raphael, in a surprisingly dashing Harlequin costume, left the backstage area and stood in the shadows outside the ring.

I pressed close to the gap in the curtain to watch the last and most dangerous act.

32

Luella and Mama took their places on either side of the dangling aerial silk. They posed like magician's assistants, resplendent in feathers and sequins. Though I could not see their faces, in their posture they were mirror images of each other: like mother, like daughter.

Above them, the aerialist climbed the silk without a single sign of fear.

I couldn't help but ball my hands until my nails bit into my palms.

The last time I saw this ...

No, I wouldn't think about that. Surely nothing could get past the combined vigilance of Luella, Mama, Raphael, and Oliver—and the rest of us, if our collective will alone could keep the aerialist aloft.

She spun and posed with seemingly effortless skill. Although I hadn't the knowledge to distinguish all the tricks by name, I knew enough to recognize certain poses.

The split balance—a split in midair, held by sheer muscle power—made me wince every single time.

In other positions, her wind magic filled the trailing silks and blew them into the shape of giant wings.

Hurry up, I urged, silently willing the music to come to a conclusion. *Get it over with already.*

But it went on, as leisurely as the silks billowed in the aerialist's magical breeze.

I think all of us backstage had stopped breathing by the time the music finally came to a triumphant conclusion. The aerialist dismounted with a slow, windmilling spin that brought her within reach of the floor. Her feet touched the ground.

Safe.

Relief flooded me with the same rush as a glass of wine on an empty stomach.

We did it. We protected the Circus Aetherium through its entire show. With any luck, we had made up for the loss of the first show, and repaired their reputation in the process.

Someone gave me a ferocious hug from behind—Pepper, of course. "I just got my ability to breathe back, Pepper, you think I could maybe keep it?"

She released me. "Sorry! I was just so relieved."

I inhaled and exhaled. "Me, too."

Tuesday ran up and pressed one dance ribbon into my hand, and one in Pepper's. "Come on, witches—time to take your bows!"

We followed her to the ring where the rest of the witches gathered under the spotlights. With the stress of the performance behind me, my blood pulsed with adrenalin, and I couldn't stop smiling. I waved the dance ribbon in jaunty patterns as the Circus Aetherium witches took their bows.

Tuesday herded the Sparkle Beach witches into a line and directed us to take our own bow—all of us, from Luella and her mother, to Oliver and Raphael, and finally Queenie, Pepper, and me.

All of us ... except Mrs. Millefleur.

My smile faltered. Where had she gone? She wasn't in our line. Nor was she at her station. I looked to Oliver.

He was already scanning the audience. A look of concern creased his brow.

I caught his eye and mouthed *Hilda*, accompanied by a gesture of empty hands.

He immediately extricated himself from the line and headed for the main tent flap.

I cast my dance ribbon aside and ran after him. The sound of the crowd's final applause roared in my ears, then faded as I emerged into the cool night.

Oliver tore off his top hat. "Damn that woman. I told her to stay close until we were done."

"Maybe she had to go get something?"

"You don't believe that any more than I do."

I surveyed the surroundings. "She must have slipped out earlier."

"If she had been wearing her necklace—"

My fingers touched the chain. "I didn't think—"

Oliver waved away my apology. "It's all right. She chose to give it to you. She had her reasons."

I frowned. "She gave me her magic, too."

"Her necklace. Her magic. And now she's gone off to who knows where." He pushed his fingers over his hair. "I don't like this."

The crowd flowed out of the tent. Oliver and I walked around the curve of the tent walls until we were out of sight of the departing spectators.

"Oliver, you don't think she—" I pressed a hand to my mouth. The thought disturbed me too much to finish.

"Go on."

"You don't think she went to her sister, do you?"

"To do what? She doesn't have any magic left to fight her with."

"That's just it. No necklace. No magic. Nothing Lenore could steal. *Nothing left to lose.* Maybe she decided to confront her, once and for all. Can you sense anyone out there?"

Oliver turned his hands palm down. A flash of silver outlined them, then went dark. "Nothing. You?"

I shook my head. "If she's out there, she's too far for me to sense."

"Maybe she took the car." He led the way to a nearby row—but the Town Car was still there.

Oliver opened the passenger side door. A piece of Millefleur Properties stationery lay on the seat. He picked it up, and his expression changed from concern to alarm. "Oh, no ..." His voice turned soft. "Hilda, you headstrong witch. What have you gotten yourself into?" He handed me the paper.

It read: *Don't follow me. I will handle this myself.*

"Of course she would pull something like this." The annoyance in my voice was only a thin veneer for the worry that crawled up my spine. "Come on. We need to get everybody." I pushed on a loose flap on the side of the tent and slipped inside.

Oliver followed me, carrying his top hat.

We dodged the lingering audience members and entered the ring. The Circus Aetherium witches were posing for pictures with admirers. We rounded up the Sparkle Beach witches—Pepper briefly protested, wanting to stay and pose for more photos—and gave them a rundown of the situation.

"Sounds like Hilda," said Mama. "Taking risks, and to hell with the consequences."

"And she never bothers to tell anyone her plans," added Oliver.

"Horatio found Mrs. Millefleur that day," I said. "Maybe he could find her again."

Luella frowned. "You said she's not nearby, though. Horatio won't necessarily follow a road to get to wherever she is. You were on foot that day, remember?"

I snapped my fingers. "You could fly after him. Like when we caught Oliver. No offense, Oliver."

"None taken," he replied. "But I dislike the idea of your friend flying headlong into possible danger." He met Raphael's gaze, and Raphael nodded in agreement.

"I got a solution for that, old tea-and-crumpets," said Mama. "You go with her."

"My talents are extensive, madam—but alas, I cannot fly."

"You don't need to." Queenie shook her head, making the ostrich feather on her turban swing from side to side. "Call up your familiar."

"My familiar?"

"He is large enough to ride," said Queenie.

Mama and Queenie stared expectantly at Oliver.

"I beg your pardon, but—"

Mama rolled her eyes. "Don't be so gosh-darned precious. Horatio will track Hilda. Luella will fly after Horatio. You follow Luella on your big old bear. The rest of us will get there as soon as you send us a location."

"I'm riding with Oliver," I hastily put in.

"Rose—" he protested.

I cut him off with a look that indicated I would sooner set his hair on fire than back down.

He met my gaze with a half smile. "Who am I to argue with a fire witch?"

Luella looked down at her costume. "Should we change?"

"No time," said Mama. "Tuesday will understand. Or, leastaways, she'll understand when Hilda writes her a check for any damages." She cackled.

We split into two groups. Mama, Queenie, Raphael, and Pepper headed for the parking lot, and Luella, Oliver, and I headed out the back, where we wouldn't be observed.

I summoned Horatio and gave him an encouraging scratch behind the ears.

Oliver called up Arthur. The bear emerged from the ground and shook off great flying cascades of sand. Oliver patted him soundly on the back. "Hello, old chap. Fancy a bit of a run?"

"You've done this before, haven't you?" I said.

"Don't tell anyone," he said. "You'll ruin my dignified image." He climbed onto the bear, then offered me a hand.

I took it and climbed up behind him. "Luella, you ready?"

She unfurled her bright silvery wings to their full length, and called up Zephyr, who arrived with her customary gust of wind.

I gripped Oliver's waist and addressed Horatio. "Okay, fire kitty, do your stuff. Find Mrs. Millefleur."

Horatio shot away. His fiery taillight bobbed in the darkness.

Luella and Zephyr flew after him.

I had only a moment to brace myself before Arthur launched forward beneath me.

33

The bear's paws flew across the sand. We bounced in rhythm with his up-and-down gait. The wild dash carried us into the scrubland surrounding the fairgrounds, where branches loomed, silhouetted by moonlight.

I tucked my head lower. "Hey, Oliver? Can you tell your bear to watch out for trees? I would appreciate not being clotheslined."

"Nonsense. People pay good money to be whipped with branches in a spa. Consider it a complimentary treatment."

I held on tighter. Oliver's top hat was long gone, abandoned back at the circus, and the scent of his hair drew me closer. Though we rode toward possible danger, my skin prickled with exhilaration.

"I find it curious," he added, "that your feline friend can follow Mrs. Millefleur."

I would have shrugged, but it wasn't a movement one could make while hanging on for dear life. "Maybe he likes fire witches."

Oliver chuckled. Pressed against him as I was, the amusement reverberated through me. "Maybe it's because you're so similar," he said.

I almost let go. "I am not similar to Hildegarde Millefleur."

"You think not?" Oliver shifted as the bear veered to the left. "Hilda is headstrong, intelligent, ambitious—"

I scoffed. "Not to mention imperious, bossy, dangerous—"

"I find you tremendously dangerous."

"Shut up, tea-and-crumpets, or I'll squeeze you till you cry for mercy."

"Is that a promise?"

Instead of responding, I rested my head against his back, letting the wind whip my hair. When I looked up, the landscape had changed. The scrubland gave way to pine trees in every direction. "Where are we?"

"Due east of the fairgrounds."

I imagined our location as if viewing it from above. "If we go any farther, there won't be any roads where the other witches can reach us. We'll be too deep in the woods."

"Do you want to turn back?"

"No—if Horatio thinks she's this far out here, that's all the more reason to find her." I couldn't see Horatio, but I could see Luella's wings, shedding copious silvery glitter, as she glided ahead.

A few minutes later, she pulled up, hovered, then dropped to the ground. Her wings retracted.

Arthur skidded to a stop. I gripped Oliver and pressed my legs against the bear's flanks in an attempt to not be hurled to the ground by the momentum.

Zephyr and Horatio sat nearby.

"Horatio stopped," Luella said.

Oliver's gaze fixed on something in the distance. "Bloody hell," he said.

I peered through the trees.

In a clearing ahead of us, a group of stone columns rose to mismatched heights. Vines dripping with flowers enveloped the columns like long, leafy fingers.

"What is that?" Oliver said. "Some kind of ruin?" He dismounted and held out his hand to assist me.

I slid down from Arthur's furry back and tugged my costume into place. "There are ruins all over Nautilus County, from people who lived here a long time ago. A lot of the sites aren't even mapped."

Luella took out her phone. "I can't get a signal."

"Can you use your air magic to tell your mom approximately where we are?"

Luella nodded.

Oliver ruffled the bear's ears. I expected him to dismiss his familiar, but he made no move to send the bear away.

The three of us walked forward slowly with our familiars by our sides.

Luella wrinkled her nose. "Smells like rotten eggs out here."

I said nothing. I was too busy feeling for heat signatures. "Hold on—" My hands went out to stop Oliver and Luella in their tracks. "There's something… cold." I cast my awareness in the direction of the coldness.

Then, I recognized it. *Water.* Like what I'd felt while walking in the woods near Izzy's, except not underground. "There's a spring in that clearing. The columns must be some old structure around it."

Except there was something else.

A faint warmth pulsed from within the cold.

"Oh, my God." I took off running. Oliver and Luella called out to me, but I didn't stop. Only Horatio kept up, his paws flying as we covered the distance. The smell of sulfur filled my nostrils. I stumbled through the stone columns and fell to my knees beside a glassy pool lit with moonlight.

Mrs. Millefleur lay face up, half in and half out of the water, her fine red suit completely soaked. Mud and twigs marred her usually perfect hair. With her eyes closed, her face lost some of its daunting fierceness. Her chest rose and fell.

I cradled her head. "Mrs. Millefleur!"

She didn't respond.

"Mrs. Millefleur, wake up!" I tried to tug her to drier ground, but couldn't.

Oliver and Luella ran up.

"Help me get her out of the water," I said.

"Stand back," said Oliver.

The earth beneath Mrs. Millefleur boiled into motion like a conveyor belt. The tumbling soil carried her away from the water's edge to drier ground. Oliver removed his jacket, rolled it up, and tucked it under her head like a pillow.

"She's soaking wet," said Luella. "She could be in shock. We need to get her dry and warm."

I kneeled beside the unconscious witch. "Come on, Mrs. Millefleur." I shook her shoulders and patted her cool cheek. I chafed her icy hands.

Nothing.

I sat back on my heels. This called for more desperate measures. "Hilda! It's me, Rose! You know you hate it when I call you by your first name."

Her eyelids fluttered.

I leaned closer. "Hilda...come on, Hilda."

A glint of light caught in her eyes, which had opened to tiny slits. "Call...me...Mrs...Millefleur."

I grinned. "Hang on to your pearls. I'm going to get you warmed up." I stretched my hands toward her body and concentrated. I couldn't collect the water, not like Pepper could, but I could toast it out of her clothing to get rid of the clammy chill.

Horatio tip-toed around me and carefully climbed onto Mrs. Millefleur's chest. He settled in place like the Sphinx and flicked his fiery tail from side to side.

Heat trickled through me. Steam rose from her clothing.

She groped in my direction, found my arm, and squeezed it with surprising strength. "Rose ..."

I leaned in, still concentrating on evaporating the water. "Yes?"

She spoke with effort. "My sister—be careful—she may still be nearby."

"What did she do to you?" asked Oliver, with dangerous calm.

Her eyes closed and her lips curved in a wry smile. "What do sisters always do?"

"Love each other, preferably?" I picked up her wrist to feel for her pulse.

The elder witch took a deep breath and let out a sigh. "We argued."

"No kidding." Her pulse was strong and steady.

"She did something to me. Tried to take my powers." She managed a weak laugh. "Knocked me out instead."

I laid her arm across her body, tucked against Horatio for extra warmth. "She's gone now, though. You're safe."

Hilda shook her head. "Look with your fire."

"First we'll get you nice and toasty."

She struggled to sit up. "Don't patronize me. I'm fine."

I blocked her with a hand on her shoulder. "You are not fine. Unless you want to be tied to a bear and galloped to the nearest hospital, I suggest you lie down and let me finish drying you off."

She complied with a disgruntled look.

It took a few minutes to evaporate the rest of the water from her clothing. When I was done, I heated the fabric until it was as warm as if it had come out of the dryer. Too bad it smelled like I'd used a rotten egg as a dryer sheet. I lifted Horatio to my shoulders and stood up. Then I offered Mrs. Millefleur a hand.

She took it and carefully got to her feet.

Luella placed her arm protectively around Mrs. Millefleur.

Mrs. Millefleur visibly flinched, and something like guilt flashed across her face. "You don't need to hold me up, Luella—"

"Nonsense." Luella gave her a little shake. "We can't have Sparkle Beach witches falling down on the job."

For once, Mrs. Millefleur seemed at a loss for words. "Well—thank you very much, I'm sure."

With that situation under control, I closed my eyes and concentrated on seeing with my fire magic. It was easy to sense the people around me—Oliver, Luella, and Mrs. Millefleur—but I was a little tired from drying Mrs. Millefleur, and it took more power to push outward in range.

"Rose—" said Oliver.

"Hang on."

"No, really—"

I opened my eyes, prepared to fire off a rebuke to the interruption, when I saw why he was interrupting me.

A woman stood on the other side of the spring, about thirty feet away, framed by two coquina columns. She set a camping lantern on a toppled column that extended into the spring-fed pool. The lantern sent orange highlights dancing across the water. With her hands free, she did a slow clap. Then she stepped into the clear space at the edge of the pool.

"I told you she wasn't gone," said Mrs. Millefleur.

Lenore wore a hooded jacket that blended with the night shadows. A bright gray streak blazed through the brown hair that peeked from under the hood. Her leggings ended in boots suitable for the outdoors, unlike the dressier pair I wore with the circus costume. She resembled Hilda, in a way, but ruggedly, with an ease that suggested she was at home in the wilderness.

With a casual movement, she flipped the hood back, revealing the rest of her hair, which had been gathered into a braid crown studded with a metallic oval hair ornament.

The shape and position of it made it resemble a third eye. Her actual eyes twinkled with something like amusement as she looked at each of us in turn. "I didn't expect you to bring the circus to me."

Luella put her hands on her hips. "How could you leave your sister like this? She could have rolled the wrong way and drowned."

Lenore laughed. Unlike Mrs. Millefleur's cultivated, musical laugh, Lenore's laugh was rich and warm, with just enough roughness to give it character. "You think I would have killed my own sister?"

"You certainly came close with that aerialist," said Oliver.

Lenore raised one eyebrow. "We all make mistakes."

"You weren't making a mistake," said Mrs. Millefleur. "You were intentionally trying to steal their powers when you thought you couldn't get mine."

"I had no way of knowing it would make them *fall over*," countered Lenore. She tapped the ornament on her braid crown. "This thing didn't exactly come with instructions on the package."

Mrs. Millefleur threw her hands up. "Exactly why you shouldn't be meddling with it."

Lenore pointed at her sister and looked to the rest of us for backup. "See? You'd knock her out, too, if you had to deal with this."

I held up my hands. "Enough! Lenore, what do you want?"

Lenore lowered her hand. "I want to do you a favor."

"I don't like favors that involve attacking my friends."

"What about your enemies?"

"What enemies? Other than you, that is."

She shook her head like it was all a misunderstanding. "Would an enemy offer you this?" Out of the inner pocket of her jacket, she drew a small cloth bag. She opened it and upended the contents into her hand.

Gold glittered in the lantern light. A few pieces of jewelry overflowed Lenore's palm and fell to the ground. She let them lie as if they were no more valuable than a dropped penny.

"See this?" She made a fist around the treasure and held it aloft. "I can give you a hundred times this amount."

"For what?"

"For your magic. I'm not truly a witch. You know that—no doubt my sister has already told you—but this little trinket can absorb magic, to be used later." She tapped the hair ornament. "The only catch is that the magic must be given freely. Trying to take it by force doesn't work, and attempting to do so apparently knocks out the witch." She gestured at our outfits. "As we all discovered during the first show."

"None of us are going to give you any magic," said Luella.

"You might not," said Lenore, "and he might not, but I haven't finished talking to Rose yet, have I?"

"I think you have," I said.

Lenore rolled her eyes. "Is she always this difficult?" she asked her sister.

Mrs. Millefleur pressed her lips together, obviously torn between wanting to say yes, and not wanting to give Lenore the satisfaction.

"Imagine it," said Lenore. "Your house completely paid off. No more working two jobs. Money to help your sister, if she needs it."

"How do you know about that?"

"I know a lot."

It was hard to look away from all the sparkling gold. "Forget it. I wouldn't give up my magic for money."

Lenore let the rest of the gold trickle through her fingers. It hit the ground at her feet. "Oh, well," she said. "It was worth a try." When she shifted her weight, her foot crushed some of the valuables, but she didn't seem to notice.

"Why do you want magic so much, anyway?"

Lenore looked at me in disbelief. "Why?" She leaned against the fallen column and cast a glance at the sky as if imploring the heavens for patience. "You know the answer. The fact that you won't give your magic up proves it. Once you get a taste of magic, you can't let it go." She shifted, and a shadow partially obscured her face. "Besides, you 'witches' use your magic for literal circus tricks rather than put it to good use. You waste it. You have no ambition. You could be out there doing *anything you want*—and instead you're flitting around like it's playtime."

"That's not true." I wanted to prove her wrong, but I had no desire to add personal details to whatever she already knew. "I've used my magic to help my family."

"So you have," she said. "Perhaps I might have something you want, after all."

I didn't like the sound of that.

Lenore pushed off from the column. "Pardon me for a moment." With that, she vanished. One moment she had been standing wreathed in shadows; the next moment, she was gone like she'd never been there at all.

I looked around. "Where did she go?"

We scanned the trees surrounding the spring.

Then, I sensed something behind me. I whipped around.

"Surprise," said Lenore. She leaned out from behind a tree and gave a little wave, then vanished again.

"How is she doing that?" I turned in a circle, bracing for her to pop up again.

And she did, about one tense minute later—on the other side of the spring. "Neat, isn't it? They call it 'the shadows.'" She made a sweeping gesture. "A literal shadow world, right under our noses, that no one can see."

"The shadows are nothing but a rumor," said Oliver.

"Are they?" said Lenore. "I'm glad you were here to fill me in on that."

"Um, hello?" I said. "Anyone want to fill me in? What shadows?"

Mrs. Millefleur narrowed her eyes at her sister. "The shadows are supposed to be a parallel dimension made of magic. The idea has been bandied about for years, but never proven."

"Until now," said Lenore. She picked up a rock and held it in the air. "Fun fact: You can put something into the shadows as easy as you can toss something into a spring." She threw the rock into the water. It made a small splash and disappeared. "Doesn't matter what it is. Rocks … or people."

Hair stood up on the back of my neck. "What do you mean, 'people'?"

Lenore smiled like we were old friends sharing a laugh over a glass of wine. "See? I told you we weren't finished talking."

34

Lenore settled herself comfortably on a weathered chunk of coquina. "Didn't you wonder why your brother-in-law—pardon me, your soon-to-be *ex*-brother-in-law—suddenly disappeared?" She peered across the small pond and a little smile lifted the corners of her lips. "I've put your troublesome brother-in-law into the shadows."

My jaw dropped. "You did *what* now?"

"Do I have to demonstrate again?" Lenore sighed and fished a stray gold chain out of the dirt. She pointed to it. "Your brother-in-law." She pointed to the spring. "The shadows." She pitched the necklace into the spring. "Ta-da!"

I pressed my fingertips to my temples. It was a shame I'd left my Advil at home. "So, let me get this straight. You kidnapped my brother-in-law and imprisoned him in a parallel dimension—made of magic—that may or may not exist. Color me unconvinced."

"What's not convincing? I went to your sister's house. I put your brother-in-law into the shadows—well, first I accidentally fired off some water magic; like I said, this thing didn't come with a manual—and I left him there. He can stay there, if you like. No more property battle." She looked pleased with herself.

Luella and I traded a look. *The water.*

"I thought you didn't like killing people," said Oliver.

Lenore shifted her gaze briefly to Oliver. "I'd make an exception for her brother-in-law. From what I know, it's not like he would be a great loss."

"Why would leaving him in the shadows kill him?" said Luella.

"Because there's nothing to eat or drink in the shadows," Lenore replied. "Save for what you bring in."

"Hold on a minute," I said. "Just because I think he's a jerk, doesn't mean I want him dead."

"Are you sure?" said Lenore. "Seems like it would solve a lot of problems. Heck, maybe he's got life insurance the kiddies can inherit."

As enjoyable as it had been to imagine Damon's ashes trampled by a herd of hippos, now that the equivalent opportunity presented itself, it didn't sound quite as fun. "I still don't have any reason to believe you actually kidnapped Damon. For all I know, this is just some wild ruse. He's probably sipping mai tais at his new bachelor condo right now."

Lenore made a tsk-tsking sound. "That reminds me. I forgot to give him any water today. You think he'll be all right until tomorrow?"

Was she lying? There was only one way to find out fast. I threaded a filament of fire magic across the water and touched Lenore's mind.

Lenore sat up straight like she'd caught me with my hand in the cookie jar. "Are you poking around in my head?"

I froze.

Having caught me, she relaxed. "Go ahead. You'll see I'm not lying—but don't push it. If I feel you going too far, I'll drop you where you stand."

I carefully sought Damon in Lenore's mind.

In her memory, his ponytail was undone and his hair straggled over his shoulders. The trees that surrounded him had no color, only the silvery tones of an old black-and-white film. He had wrapped his arms around his knees and laid his head on his arms. The eerie silence made my hands go cold.

I shivered and withdrew the magic. "Take me to him."

"He's right here."

"Prove it."

"Mind-reading not enough for you?" Lenore sighed and got to her feet. "Fine. But I can't have your friends making trouble while I'm gone."

My hand shot out. "Lenore, wait—"

She touched the ornament on her braid and made three sharp tugs in mid-air with her other hand. With each tug, one of my friends dropped to the ground.

I sank to the ground, trying and failing to revive them. They were all breathing, thank God, but they wouldn't wake. Fury filled me. "You didn't have to do that!"

"Sorry," she said. "But don't worry—they're unharmed. You saw what happened at the circus." She shook her head, as if chastising herself for her own mistake. "You can't take a witch's powers, but you sure can knock them out." With that observation, she winked out of sight—one moment there, one moment gone.

I slammed my fists to the ground. I was the true witch in this situation, but what good were my powers if Lenore could disable any witch, any time she pleased?

I gripped the fire opal until it hurt my palm. My head bowed—and an herbal aroma cut through the reek of the sulfur spring: the sage I'd pinned to my costume for luck. I inhaled, letting the sharp scent clear my head.

Beside me, Zephyr nudged Luella with her nose. She waved her fluffy tail in half-hearted confusion, as if Luella might be playing some new, unknown game. Arthur sank to his large hindquarters beside Oliver and looked as forlorn as a bear could look.

Horatio pushed his head under my hand. His warm fur brought me comfort, and lifted my heavy heart, just as the sage had cleared my head. His insistent meow brought me firmly back to myself.

I stroked his head. "Thank you, fire kitty."

Lenore had a magical trinket that let her pretend to be a witch, but she didn't have what I had. She didn't come here with friends. She wasn't fighting for someone she loved. She worked alone. She would have bought me off, or threatened me—whatever it took—to get what she wanted. With tactics like that, she had isolated herself.

All she had was gold and threats.

But I had something more.

"Rose." Lenore's voice carried across the pond and interrupted my reverie.

I lifted my head. Next to Lenore stood Damon, looking pale and disoriented, with his slouchy linen shirt askew.

"Here he is." She touched him with one finger and he vanished, presumably back into the gray shadow world I'd seen in Lenore's mind. "And there he goes. What'll it be? Shall I leave him in there, or do you want him back?" She said this in a friendly way, like she was presenting a choice of hamburger or hot dog at a company picnic.

Lenore would get what she wanted whether she got rid of him or let him go free. If the situation weren't so dire, I could have better appreciated the elegant trap—and the strange, dark humor of the person who'd thought of it.

I needed to keep her on the hook and make her believe I would really give up my magic. I was no actor, but—like it or not—the bank of a sulfurous abandoned spring was my stage. "If I give you my magic, you'll let him go?"

"If that's what you want. Personally, I think everyone would be better off without him, but ..." She shrugged.

I made a show of regarding my friends, who remained motionless on the ground. "And you'll leave us alone?"

"I only came back for my sister's magic. If she had done what she promised, I wouldn't be here at all."

"That's not an answer."

"It's the answer I'm giving."

All that mattered was that I got that damned artifact away from her. Time to earn that Oscar. I hung my head like I was defeated, then looked up again with what I hoped was a convincing appearance of resignation. "Let him go, and I'll give you what you want."

Lenore flashed out of sight and reappeared with a disoriented-looking Damon. She gave him a playful shove. "Off you go."

Damon staggered around to my side of the spring, and collapsed against a tree with a groan.

At least he was out of the way, and relatively unharmed. I faced Lenore. "How do I give you my magic?"

"Simple as pie. Send it to me willingly, and I'll catch it."

"Okay." I shook out my arms. "Here it comes."

Now came the tricky part.

Assuming that she could sense incoming magic in some rudimentary way, I'd have to feed her enough of it to make her believe her plan was working—while also enacting my own plan. Oliver had cautioned us about magic and multitasking, but I'd just have to be good enough to pull it off.

I reached out with the thinnest possible thread of fire magic. It snaked its silvery way across the pond and connected with the artifact she wore in her hair.

Her face lit up. "Yes, that's it!'

While I kept that thread going, I pushed a second thread of magic to Mrs. Millefleur. With the connection in place, I released the powers she'd pressed upon me. While the fire magic trickled slowly and steadily between us, Mrs. Millefleur's unconscious mind was a starry sky on a cloudless night. I could see anything I wanted to—but there was only one thing I was looking for.

Her familiar.

I'd seen it, although I didn't know it at the time, on that very first day when Mrs. Millefleur showed up at my door. I'd spotted it again, unknowingly, on the day she taught me in the forest.

Small, fast—and typically found running along fences or tree branches.

If all of the familiars would obey me, I had an advantage Lenore would never be able to see coming—but everything depended on whether or not I could coax Mrs. Millefleur's familiar out of hiding.

I called to the small, fiery creature I sensed hiding in the trees: *Come out and play, little squirrel.*

The ball of heat scampered down. I knew without looking that it had crossed the open ground; when it stopped, I could sense it near Mrs. Millefleur.

I hid my smile with a frown, though Lenore was probably too busy greedily absorbing the tiny flow of power to notice my facial expression.

The squirrel crept in front of me. It twitched its brown bottlebrush tail like a furry race car revving its engine. Then it looked up at me, ready for a command, its gaze oddly solemn for such a fun-sized creature.

I met its gaze. *Fire squirrel, you have the most important job. You must get the jewel from her hair and bring it to me.*

The squirrel spun around, faced across the pond, and crouched low. Then its fluffy tail burst into silver flames.

It was ready.

Now for the other familiars.

Arthur, Zephyr, Horatio, I thought. *Tackle Lenore on my signal. Do not let her touch the gem on her head.*

The great bear and the white-and-silver dog came to my side, next to Horatio.

I took one more look over my shoulder at my friends, still unconscious on the ground, and Damon, insensible against a tree.

I squared my shoulders. It was all on me—and the familiars I commanded by the gift of trust from my friends.

We were ready.

One last word—one last thought—to set it all in motion: *Go!*

The familiars dashed across the water with the fire squirrel in the lead.

Lenore, not being a real witch, did not see them coming. She barely had time to squeak in surprise when Zephyr and Arthur knocked her down and pinned her to the ground. Horatio added his weight to the pile-on, hissing triumphantly.

Mrs. Millefleur's familiar—the only one with paws tiny and clever enough to do what needed to be done—was a blur of motion on Lenore's braid crown. It pulled the hair ornament free and scampered back across the water with it clenched in its teeth.

The squirrel stopped at my feet, removed the ornament, and held it up in its paws.

"Good squirrel." I took the gem. "Horatio! Zephyr and Arthur!"

The rest of the familiars retreated across the water, leaving Lenore flat on her back on the other bank of the spring. Zephyr returned to guard Luella, and Arthur stood watch over Oliver. The feisty fire squirrel sat on Mrs. Millefleur's ankle and let out a stream of furious chatter.

I held the artifact in my palm. Up close, it wasn't just shaped like an eye—it gave the disconcerting impression that it was, in fact, staring at you. I closed my fingers over it. There wasn't time to examine it fully. I couldn't take the chance of letting such a dangerous item fall into Lenore's hands again. I held it up and aimed for the boil.

Lenore pushed herself upright. "Rose, wait! You don't know what that artifact means to me. You don't know what I've been through."

"You're right. I don't know." I lowered my arm. "And—*I don't care*. The next time you think about crashing my town, Lenore?" I flipped the artifact in the air like a quarter and caught it. "Think again."

Then I threw the artifact into the center of the spring.

35

"No!" cried Lenore. She ripped off her jacket and threw her boots aside. She took a running jump into the pool, where she sank out of sight, leaving behind ripples of agitated water. Her feet briefly broke the surface when she kicked to dive deeper.

While she splashed and thrashed in the spring, I turned my attention to Mrs. Millefleur, Luella, and Oliver. "Wake up." I shook their shoulders in turn, and rubbed their hands. It took a minute or two, but at last they came around to the sound of Lenore flailing in the water.

Mrs. Millefleur sat up and gingerly patted her hair, as if to assess the damage. "What is going on?" She blinked in the direction of the spring.

Lenore surfaced and gasped for air.

"Lenore, get out of that water this instant before you catch your death," said Mrs. Millefleur.

Lenore moved her arms to stay afloat despite the clothing weighing her down. "You're not my mother." She dove under the water again.

Oliver sat up and put his arm over Arthur, then used the leverage to pull himself to a standing position. "Rose, why is Mrs. Millefleur's sister going swimming?"

"I threw her artifact in the boil."

"Oh." He caught sight of Damon. "And is that your ne'er-do-well brother-in-law?"

"Soon to be 'ex,'" I said. I helped Luella stand. "Are you all right?"

"Better than she is, I think," she replied, nodding toward the spring.

Lenore bobbed to the surface. Rivulets of water ran from her sodden braid crown down her face. "I'm too old to start over," she said, her voice ringing with frustration. "Do you know what it's like out there for a woman in her sixties?"

"I *am* a woman in my sixties, thank you very much," said Mrs. Millefleur. "I know exactly what it's like." Her face softened. "Come home, Lenore. We can make this right."

Lenore's eyes flashed in the lantern light. "Don't you dare feel sorry for me." With that, she ducked beneath the surface and kicked her way into the depths of the spring.

Dozens of bubbles broke the surface.

"How long can she stay down there?" said Oliver.

The bubble slowed to a handful.

Mrs. Millefleur hastened to the water's edge. "Lenore?"

Oliver, Luella, and I joined her.

"Don't fall in," I said. "I don't want to have to dry you out twice in one day." But the humor rang hollow as seconds ticked by and Lenore did not emerge.

The bubbles stopped.

"Lenore!" Mrs. Millefleur's face tightened with real fear as she gazed into the black water. She tore off her red jacket and was starting to kick off her shoes when Luella and Oliver grabbed her by the arms. "Let me go!" she cried.

Where was Lenore? I plunged my magic into the cold spring—searching left, right, and down—nothing. Not even a hint of heat. Not even if the worst had happened would the water have turned so uniformly cold again, so quickly.

Lenore had disappeared.

"She's gone," I said.

"What do you mean, gone?" said Mrs. Millefleur.

"She's vanished. She was in the water, and now she's not." I swept the surrounding area using my heat sensitivity to look for anything person-sized. I found only Damon, still propped against a tree, muttering to himself. "Look for yourself."

Mrs. Millefleur blinked. "What do you mean?"

"Haven't you noticed?"

Her eyes widened. She looked at her hand. A tiny silver flame danced from finger to finger. She stared at me for a long moment. "You … you gave me my magic back. After everything that happened—after what I did—"

"You can make it up to me by making a habit of telling me what's going on, rather than running off into the woods alone."

"I'll do my best." Mrs. Millefleur spread her hands toward the spring. Her wrinkles creased with concentration. Faint silver sparks glimmered over the water. Then she lowered her hands, and the sparks winked out. "She *is* gone. How is that possible?" she said.

"The shadows," said Luella, in a hushed voice.

"But I took her artifact …" I shoved my fingers into my hair as if the painful tug would produce a sensible explanation.

Mrs. Millefleur shook her head. "She's my sister. She must have had a backup plan."

The squirrel, who had run off when Mrs. Millefleur woke up, charged out of its hiding place and greeted us with a series of scolding noises.

The other familiars pricked up their ears.

"Look who's here, Mrs. Millefleur," I said. "I think someone wanted to see you."

She bent low and picked up the squirrel. It ran up her arm and perched on her shoulder with a satisfied chitter. "I suppose I can't keep you hidden anymore, can I?" she said.

"What's its name?" said Luella.

"Chuck. After my late husband." Mrs. Millefleur tickled the squirrel under its chin. "And, Rose?" She paused and looked me in the eye. "Call me Hilda." She walked away to the other side of the pool. Oliver followed her. Together, they picked the fallen gold out of the dirt one piece at a time.

Luella grabbed my shoulders. "Are you all right?"

"I'm fine."

"I doubt it," she said. "It's not easy to face someone powerful who means you harm."

"You would know."

She smiled. "It doesn't always turn out how you think it will."

I surveyed the scene: the chair of the Downtown Merchant Association with a fire squirrel on her shoulder; a chauffeur trailed by a shuffling bear; my best friend looking like she was on her way to *carnaval*, and—where was Damon?

I sure as hell hadn't saved him only to lose him again.

"Damon's gone," I said. I reached with my magic to find any large heat signatures moving into the distance. From what I could tell, he had barely moved away from the spring. "He's not far. I can catch him."

"Do you want me to come?" said Luella.

"It's just Damon. I can handle him."

Horatio ran along with me as I jogged in the direction where I estimated Damon to be. He was navigating more or less blind, whereas I could sense both his location and the location of my friends back at the spring. It made me feel far more comfortable sprinting into the dark.

I heard his winded puffs and clumsy blundering before I saw him. "Damon!"

He continued dragging himself forward, clutching at trees for support as he went.

I judged the distance between us and shot a precise line of magical fire in front of him.

The ground ignited and burned. Damon shied back, then turned to face me with his hands up.

"Rose, whatever you're mixed up in, I don't want any part of it. Just—just let me go, okay? Please don't put me back in there."

I clenched my hand to extinguish the fire—I had no desire to burn the forest down. The motion made him flinch. "Calm down. I'm not putting you anywhere."

Horatio sat by my feet and added a small yowl to this statement.

"I'll give Izzy the house," he said. "She and the girls can have it."

Ah, there was that champagne feeling again. And this time, it was for real. "You don't want it anymore?"

He slid down against a tree and hung his head. "You don't know what it was like. I—I thought that woman wasn't going to let me out. I thought I might never see Astrid and Sadie again."

I crouched beside him. I didn't need to read his mind; the haunted look on his face told me he was telling the truth. "Will you tell me about what happened? Not now, I mean. When you've recovered."

He nodded.

"Let's get you out of here." I stood and offered him my hand. He took it, and I helped him to his feet. He leaned on me to walk. "You know you can't tell anyone else about this, right?"

Damon scoffed. "I can't tell anyone because no one would believe a word of it."

"No, you can't tell anyone because then I would have to kill you."

He looked uncertain as to whether I was serious, which suited me just fine. We returned to the others. Oliver eyed Damon with a look of distaste, but took charge of him anyway, guiding him to sit down on a coquina boulder a short distance away.

I took the lamp from Mrs. Millefleur—Hilda—and walked around the spring. I held it over the water, hoping to spot the lost artifact. The golden light glittered on something large deep within the spring; whatever it was, it twisted and disappeared into the boil, beyond sight.

"Do you see anything?" called Luella.

I lowered the lamp. "Just a big fish," I said.

But I wasn't really sure.

36

I raked over the dirt in Izzy's backyard one more time, smoothing out the spots Damon had missed when he hastily filled in the apparent sinkhole. Already, the house sang inside and out with Izzy's touch, a reminder that the balance had fully shifted in her favor. I leaned on the rake and took in the sight of the flourishing plants around me. Horatio lay in a patch of sunlight and lashed his tail.

Izzy emerged from the back door carrying two steaming mugs. She handed me one.

I sipped. The hot apple cider took out some of the afternoon's chill. "I don't know how you do it," I said. "Everything is green and beautiful even in the middle of winter."

A touch of pride graced her smile. "You should come inside," she said. "Your friends will be here soon."

"I know."

Neither of us moved.

"Izzy," I said. "Does it bother you that I have magic, and you don't?"

She chuckled. "Rose, does it bother you that I have a Christmas tree up, and you don't?"

"What?" I laughed. "No. It's not my thing. I'd rather visit everyone else's. Let them do the hard work."

"Then you understand how I feel."

"Really?"

"Really. Of course, if you come up with some kind of magic that cleans houses, all bets are off."

"You'll be the first to know."

The back door banged open and Sadie poked her head out. "Someone's here!"

"That's our cue," I said.

We went inside and set down our mugs. I opened the front door to find Luella and Pepper holding a large Tupperware container between them. "Surprise!" they said, and brandished the container in my direction.

I took it and nearly staggered under the weight. "What on earth is this?"

"A twelfth cake," said Luella.

I set the cake on the bar. "Did it take that many times to get it right?"

"You're hilarious."

"I helped," said Pepper. "Well—I sampled the frosting. Does that count?"

"Cake!" shouted Sadie, to no one in particular.

The noise brought Astrid out of her bedroom. "Did somebody say, 'cake'?"

We all crowded around as Luella removed the lid and revealed a large round cake covered in elaborate frosting.

"Holy mother of sugar," I said.

Izzy retrieved a stack of plates, a cake knife, and some forks and napkins. She hummed an upbeat tune as she set them out on the table.

"Bet you're feeling good," said Pepper.

Izzy smiled. "Things are definitely looking up."

"You're not mad you missed all the excitement, are you?" Pepper winked broadly, in case Izzy had somehow managed to miss her meaning.

"What excitement?" said Sadie.

Izzy saved us from explaining by cutting the first slice and handing it to Sadie. "Here's your cake," she said.

Sadie promptly forgot all about whatever the "excitement" was. She marched out to the backyard with her cake and settled on a beach towel to dine al fresco.

Astrid snagged the next piece and shuffled back to her room, in true teenager fashion, with her headphones over her ears.

With the girls out of earshot, we could speak freely.

"I'm mad *I* missed the excitement," continued Pepper. She stabbed her fork in the direction of Luella and me. "Everybody else got to have all the fun. And if either one of you tells me my turn will come—*again*—you'll be wearing this cake."

Luella made a face of pure innocence. "Wouldn't dream of it."

Mollified, Pepper stuck her fork into the thick slice. "At least I'll be living it up this spring."

"What are you doing this spring?" asked Izzy.

"My husband and I are finally going on a vacation. Just the two of us. No kids. Honestly, I don't even remember what it's like not to be responsible for small humans twenty-four hours a day."

"See, you do get to have fun," I said.

"Not as exciting as having a magical showdown," she said. A grin bloomed on her face. "But pretty good." She took a bite of cake, then froze. Her eyes widened.

"Pepper?" said Luella. "You okay?"

Pepper made a strange expression and fished something out of her mouth. She brandished what appeared to be a large bean at Luella. "You trying to give Pete some extra work today?"

Izzy looked confused.

I nudged her. "Pepper's husband is a dentist."

"You got the bean!" said Luella. "Congratulations."

Pepper squinted at the bean. "Do I get a prize?"

"The bean is the prize," I said. "It means you're the queen."

"Yay, I'm the queen! You can be my court," she added generously.

We finished our cake while watching Sadie out the window. She danced around her beach towel with abandon.

Izzy set down her plate and clapped her hands together. "I forgot—I wanted to show you my redecorating project."

Luella, Pepper, and I followed her into the room where Damon had been sleeping. Izzy had cleared a space and assembled a tall workbench from discarded lumber and blocks.

Clear jars lined the bench from end to end, and bundles of dried flowers and herbs hung from a rack on the wall.

"Do you like it? It's my new wildcrafting space."

Luella ran her hand over the surface of the workbench. "It's beautiful."

Izzy retrieved a set of three bottles filled with golden oil and sealed with wax. "These are for you. For helping me." She gave one to me, one to Pepper, and one to Luella. "It's a massage oil with ginger in it. Useful for aches and pains, or just for smelling nice. I grew the ginger myself."

We thanked her with hugs and exclamations of admiration.

After a while, Luella and Pepper had to be on their way. We said our goodbyes, and I embraced Izzy one more time before leaving her to her happy home, her wildcrafting, and her girls.

I swung into the truck with a smile. "Come on, Horatio. We have a date."

He appeared in a flash and settled himself in his customary shotgun spot.

I pulled out my phone and sent a single line of text: *I'm on my way.*

An answer returned: *I'll see you there.*

The distance flew by. The tires crunched over gravel when I pulled into the cabin driveway.

Home at last.

The white Town Car sat in the driveway. Oliver leaned against it. He wore a black sweater paired with jeans so dark-washed they were almost, but not quite, black.

I shut off the engine and hopped down with Horatio.

Oliver pushed off the Town Car. "Well met, fire witch."

"Hello there, tea-and-crumpets."

He leaned in and kissed my cheek. Even that slight touch was enough to send tendrils of electricity down my spine. I imagined them earthing into the ground beneath my feet.

We went up to the porch and entered the cabin.

Braveheart galloped up, all big paws and happy slobber. Oliver leaned down and firmly patted Braveheart's back in just the way the dog liked best. "Good boy," he said.

I put down my things and picked up the little Gothic harp I'd finally decided to purchase. Some days, I could barely keep my hands off it. It produced a bright and clear tone even in my inexperienced hands. After plucking a few strings just to hear them sing, I replaced the harp in its cradle.

Oliver observed all of this without comment, only a slight smile. Then he cleared his throat. "I have a surprise for you before we go out."

I raised my eyebrows. "I think I've had enough surprises for one season." I followed him out the back anyway, with Braveheart and Horatio on my heels.

He pivoted once we were outside, facing me and blocking my view. "Close your eyes."

I couldn't resist sneaking a look around, to no avail, before closing my eyes as requested.

Oliver took my arm and led me across the sandy ground. His heat signature glowed in my magical vision. "Open your eyes."

An elegant old-fashioned rose bush filled a previously empty corner of the yard. Bright double-petaled crimson blooms covered the bush, contrasting with the dark green leaves.

I breathed the scent. The sweet aroma was lush and full, heady and intoxicating. "Oh, Oliver—you shouldn't have."

"A rose for a rose, don't you think?"

"No, really, you shouldn't have—I kill every plant I touch …"

"Not this one. It's enchanted. I added just a touch of earth magic. Nothing short of a shovel, a fireball, or old age could take this out."

Braveheart nudged the nearest rose, shook his head till his ears flapped, then sneezed. Horatio batted at a low-hanging blossom.

I embraced Oliver. "It's beautiful. Thank you."

He carefully picked a rose, checked it for thorns, and tucked it into my hair.

With a rose in my hair, and the scent of sage still clinging to my clothes—I'd tucked some dried sprigs into my dresser drawers—contentment filled me.

We crossed the backyard to the border with the forest beyond. When we were well into the trees, Oliver summoned Arthur. The bear emerged from the forest floor and shook himself heartily, sending dried leaves tumbling back to the ground.

The five of us walked on.

"Is this a goodbye, then?" I said.

Oliver pulled up short. "What makes you say that?"

I faced him, but for some reason, I had trouble meeting his gaze. "I assumed you would move on, now that Lenore is gone, and no longer has her artifact."

"Rose—"

"I know you don't settle in one place for long. You go where there's work to be done."

"Rose, may I say something—"

"And it's okay, we're both independent people—"

He placed a fingertip on my lips.

I made as if to bite it.

He chuckled and moved his finger to stroke my cheek. "Dear Rose," he said, "there is much left to do here in Sparkle Beach. Not to mention there's this fiery, stubborn witch who keeps making my life more interesting than it ever was before."

That was enough for me. I grabbed him like I had on the day we met and planted a kiss on him that made him stagger backwards. He recovered well enough, though, and returned the kiss with equal fervor. It was fire, it was earth—and it was perfect.

Braveheart dashed around us, barking wildly.

Arthur, not to be outdone, lightly headbutted us until we broke apart, laughing.

Horatio meowed impatiently.

"That's our cue." I petted Arthur's head, then climbed onto his back.

Oliver settled behind me and wrapped his arms around me.

I leaned forward and buried my fingers in the bear's thick fur, releasing the mineral scent of freshly turned earth. "Ready?" I said.

"Ready," Oliver replied, close and warm.

"Ready, Braveheart? Ready, Horatio?"

Braveheart frolicked from sheer excitement. Horatio crouched like a coiled spring.

I squeezed the bear's flanks. "Let's go!"

We charged forward. Braveheart and Horatio dashed alongside as we raced headlong into the deep forest. The gallop stole my breath, but I couldn't stop smiling. Life was an adventure I intended to seize with both hands. With my family to ground me, and my friends to lift me up, I could do anything, *be* anything—a goth queen, a fire witch, a righter of wrongs, sometimes a lover and sometimes a loner—with the earth beneath me, the wind in my hair, and a blazing fire in my heart.

The Midlife Elementals adventure continues in

Silver Dreams!